ARE YOU EXPERIENCED?

Jordan Sonnenblick

SQUARE
FISH

Feiwel and Friends
New York

SQUARE FISH

An Imprint of Macmillan
175 Fifth Avenue
New York, NY 10010
fiercereads.com

Our books may be purchased in bulk for promotional, educational,
or business use. Please contact your local bookseller or the Macmillan
Corporate and Premium Sales Department at (800) 221-7945 ext. 5442
or by e-mail at MacmillanSpecialMarkets@macmillan.com.

Library of Congress Cataloging-in-Publication Data Available

ISBN 978-1-250-06304-5 (paperback)   ISBN 978-1-4668-4841-2 (ebook)

Originally published in the United States by Feiwel and Friends
First Square Fish Edition: 2015
Book designed by Ashley Halsey
Square Fish logo designed by Filomena Tuosto

10 9 8 7 6 5 4 3 2 1

AR: 5.3 / LEXILE: 840L

This book is dedicated to everyone who has endured childhood abuse or neglect. You can't change your past, but you can control your future.

TUESDAY, OCTOBER 21, 2014

It only takes one annoying little noise to ruin a perfectly good death scene. I was floating, bodiless, through space—or time—or some formless realm. I wasn't feeling any of the physical pains or discomforts that we all feel without noticing, not to mention the huge ones that I, in particular, should have been suffering. I wasn't even aware of the mental agony of walking away for the last time from two new, doomed friends. I felt nothing but an endless expanse of warm light all around me.

And then came the friggin' beeping, once every second or so. The sound seemed to be coming from incredibly far away, as though my head were wrapped in layers of cotton or something. I was pretty sure it had been going on for a while, gradually annoying its way into my awareness. I tried to turn my head to locate the sound, but the smallest attempt at movement made me so dizzy I decided to just be still and concentrate on my senses.

I smelled burning hair. Burning hair, and some awful mixture of cows, mud, and smoke. I wanted to open my eyes and see where in the world I could possibly be, but even through my closed eyelids, everything looked too bright to handle.

My hands. My hands were at my sides. I could feel cool fabric against the backs of my fingers, and all the way up my arms. There were cold things—tubes or wires of some sort—running along my forearms. I was in a bed. Yikes! I was in a hospital.

The beeping sped up.

"Honey, what's happening?" a frightened female voice asked. "Is he awake?"

Mom!

"Easy. Take it easy, sweetheart. You heard the doctors. His brain scans are completely flat. People with flat brain scans don't just wake up."

My father, the optimist.

All of a sudden, I was shaking and shivering all over, so hard that I could feel my teeth smashing against each other, my mouth filling with blood as my incisors slashed the inside of my left cheek. My body arched, but apparently

2

there was some kind of restraining belt across my chest that kept me from flying completely up and out of the bed.

"Nurse!" my father yelled. He was a strong yeller.

Footsteps pounding into the room, at least two sets. Too many voices for me to sort out. A clink as somebody banged what must have been an IV pole off the frame of my bed, and then a lone female voice saying, "This will settle him down. It's the strongest dosage of antiseizure medication I'm allowed to give him, at least until . . ."

Whatever drug she put into my IV must have been super fast-acting, because right in the middle of her sentence, a warm toasty feeling spread up my arm, and throughout my whole body. I'm not sure whether I stopped shaking as soon as it reached my head, but I am sure I stopped caring.

Sometime later, the beeping worked its way into my world again, along with the muffled voices of my parents. This time, I didn't even try to move. Even breathing was an effort, so I just listened. I figured they were probably talking about me. I admit, I kind of wanted to hear my parents sobbing and crying about how their only son was lying here twitching.

Dad was talking in a defeated monotone. "It was right after high school graduation. He was going to work at the steel factory in the fall, as soon as a job opened up in the welding department."

I lay there, thinking, *High school graduation? What's he talking about? I'm only fifteen. I'm a sophomore.*

"Then came the big concert and . . ."

Dad stopped talking. It almost sounded like he was too choked up to speak.

"You don't have to talk about it if you don't want to, honey," Mom said.

Dad launched right back into his tale. He's pretty abrupt. I have manners, but don't ask me where I got them from. "Do you know why I went to the concert?"

"I don't know. You've never wanted to talk about it."

"I was excited about the music, and the party aspects of it. I was fifteen—who wouldn't have been? But that wasn't the main thing. My brother had a girlfriend. She was the most beautiful thing I had ever seen. He was crazy about her. That's why what happened afterward doesn't make any sense."

He paused again. I couldn't believe this. My parents weren't talking about me at all. They weren't even thinking about me.

"Anyway, he came home one day in the beginning of August saying he had bought two tickets to this amazing music festival in New York State. I was so excited. I started talking a mile a minute about how great this was going to be. One last trip as brothers before he started his grown-up life and everything changed! That was when he laid it

4

on me: the tickets were for him and his girlfriend. I begged him to take me with them. I said I'd buy my own ticket with my lawn-mowing money. I knew Dad would kill me if he remembered to, but half the time when Dad was angry, we could just get him crocked and he would forget all about it. Anyway, it didn't seem to matter, because my brother didn't budge. He said he was really looking forward to this trip with his girlfriend, and it had to be just the two of them. I tried everything I could think of to change his mind. I argued. I yelled. I threatened to quit the band. I pouted. I refused to talk to him. But then I got really scared: What if the reason he wouldn't take me was because he wasn't planning to come back? That seemed possible. As hard as our parents were for me to deal with, they were a million times harder on my brother. They got on him for every-thing. I almost wouldn't have blamed him if he wanted to head out with his girl and just keep going."

"But you did go, honey. So what happened?"

"That's the strange part. I've never figured out why, but all of a sudden, about a week before the concert, my brother just showed up after work one day with a third ticket and told me I should start getting my camping gear together. I asked him what had changed, and all he would say is that he wanted to give me the best weekend of my life. I've spent the last four decades wondering whether I should have known what he was going to do, right then and there."

Dad stopped talking and broke down in heavy sobs. I heard a chair squeak, which must have been Mom moving closer to comfort him.

Typical.

My name is Rich Barber. If you want a snapshot of everything you need to know about the first fifteen years of my life, this is a pretty good one. I am lying in a hospital bed, while three feet away, my father can't get over something that happened forty-five years ago.

FRIDAY, AUGUST 15, 1969

They say we all come into this world naked and screaming, but most of us only have to do it once. The second time I did it, I was fifteen years old—or negative forty-five years old, depending on how you look at things. Like a newborn baby, I was immediately hit by a flash of blinding light as soon as I opened my eyes. Unlike a newborn baby, I was then hit by a Cadillac.

Fortunately, it was a pretty slow-moving Cadillac, so I only spun maybe fifteen feet through the air before landing in a nice, grassy ditch by the side of whatever road I was on. It still hurt, though. Believe me, there's no such thing as getting gently hit by a Cadillac. The car's front bumper had nailed me in the right hip, which now pulsed and throbbed with a strange kind of burning ache. I lay on my back in the ditch for a while, catching my breath, smelling the sun-warmed soil around me, feeling the vegetation against my bare skin, and wondering where the heck I was.

I was afraid to open my eyes again, because the first time hadn't gone so well. But then a shadow and a chill passed over me, and a soft voice said, "Hey, are you okay?" I couldn't help it: I looked, and forgot all about my hip for a moment. The most beautiful girl I had ever seen was kneeling over me. She had long, dark hair parted down the middle, huge brown eyes, incredibly tan skin, and a look of shocked concern on her face. She was maybe a few years older than I was, and had on some seriously weird clothing: shorts, a tie-dyed T-shirt, tons of beaded necklaces that were hanging almost down to my face, and a fringed leather vest that actually was brushing up against the skin of my chest.

BECAUSE I WAS NAKED. Holy cow.

My first rational thought was that this had to be a dream. I blinked several times really fast to see whether I would wake up. When I stopped, the beautiful girl in the retro outfit was still there, and now she was reaching down to brush my hair out of my eyes. She looked so kind and so worried that I had my second rational thought: *Good God. I'm dead! That's what this is. The blinding flash of light, the car, the flying-through-the-air part, and now this gorgeous hippie supermodel waking me up . . . it all makes sense. Now she's going to hand me a harp and a pair of wings.*

"Um," I said, "are you an angel?"

Her eyes widened. "No. I thought you were."

Wait a minute. Why would anyone think I was an angel? With great effort, I sat up. This allowed me to hunch over so I wasn't quite so exposed, which was a good thing, because as I got a look around, I realized my accident had drawn a crowd. There were tons and tons of young people in a rough circle around me, pointing and saying things like "Far out!" The bottom of the ditch was a foot or two below ground level, so I was looking up at the road. From what I could see, we were in the middle of nowhere, but for some reason, there was a massive traffic jam all around, anyway. That was probably why the Cadillac hadn't completely smeared me into the pavement. Speaking of which, it was pulled over right next to me, and two guys who were dressed pretty much like the girl were huddled alongside the passenger doors, whispering frantically to each other. One looked about her age, and I would have guessed the other one was a tenth-grader like me. If one of them had been driving when the car hit me, I wondered why they weren't using a cell phone to dial 9-1-1.

I suddenly realized another incredibly weird fact: Every single car I could see was incredibly old, but looked new. I mean, the styles of the cars were ancient. There were Volkswagen Beetles like the original Herbie the Love Bug, gigantic rectangular American muscle cars and sedans like the one that had almost killed me, Scooby-Doo-looking vans, and a wide assortment of other oldies that should have been rusted through—but somehow they all looked like they had just been freshly painted.

I had a bad feeling about this . . . a bad feeling worse than the one from an automobile smashing into my hip and flinging me into a ditch. Sweat burst out on my forehead, and I shivered despite the sun. My heart pounding, I asked the girl, "Where am I? What happened? Who are you?"

She laughed. It sounded tinkly, and I thought of birds playing xylophones. Okay, maybe I had hit my head in the fall, but even in the middle of everything, I loved the sound of her laughter. "Wow, you really must be an angel! You just, like, appeared in the road. Michael was talking to me, and I was trying to change the station on the radio, you know? So I wasn't looking up or anything. But then there was this flash, and David said, 'Look out!' I felt the bump, and there you were, all white like an angel, flying through the air."

I figured David and Michael were probably the guys having the conference by the Cadillac. "But, uh, where are we?"

She threw her head back and made with the tinkly laugh again. "This is so far out! If you're not an angel, you must at least be from another planet or something. You're the only kid for a hundred miles around who doesn't know about the festival!"

"Festival?"

"You know, the Woodstock Music and Art Fair?"

I stared at her, stunned.

"An Aquarian Exposition? Three days of peace and music?"

I kept on staring.

Another laugh. "Haven't you seen the posters all over the place?"

Oh. My. God. I had seen one of those posters. A faded, partly torn one, decades old, in a frame on the wall of my father's den.

She continued. "August fifteenth through seventeenth?"

I swallowed. My lips and throat felt very, very dry. "What . . . what year?"

"Wow," she said. "If you're an angel, you're a silly angel. It's 1969, of course. When else would it be?"

I SHALL BE RELEASED

FRIDAY, OCTOBER 17, 2014

I guess if you're looking for the real beginning of this story, this is it. The day had started out looking pretty promising. I was psyched up, because my girlfriend, Courtney, had asked me to play my guitar and sing at a protest thing outside our little town's city hall. Well, she was actually my sort-of girlfriend. I wanted to commit, but she said I was too "emotionally inexperienced." Whatever that means. We were both sophomores at the same high school, and she had reminded me about the protest all day long—in the hallways, at lunch, even via text during classes. I mean, we weren't supposed to text in class, but Courtney was not exactly a master rule-follower.

Like there was any chance I would forget. I had spent the entire week figuring out a million different protest songs on my guitar, and singing them until I thought my parents would strangle me. Actually, on any given day lately, it seemed like there was a fifty-fifty chance my parents would strangle me whether I played the guitar or not.

The thing about my parents is this: they are ancient. Seriously, seriously ancient. As in, my mom was forty-one years old when she had me, and my dad was a whopping forty-five. Do you have any idea what that's like? It means that everywhere I've gone with them my entire life, well-meaning people have said things like, "Oh, you're such a cute little boy! Are these your grandparents?" And then my parents have gotten their feelings hurt, but of course they have to act all polite in public, so they just get in a terrible mood as soon as they're alone with me.

It also means other kids notice. The first time my dad tried to pitch baseballs to my team during Little League practice, he threw out his back and had to go to the emergency room. When my mom attempted to teach me to ice-skate in front of my whole class on a grade-school trip, she fell and dislocated her hip. It took three skate guards to get her off the ice and into the ambulance. I was amazed they didn't have to call in some kind of special rescue Zamboni. In case that wasn't humiliating enough, a couple of years ago, my parents had a little ornamental pond installed in our backyard, with a tower of rocks and a pump that shoots a constant stream of water down over them. You know what my friends call it?

Viagra Falls.

Plus, I don't know if it's the massive age difference, the fact that I'm an only child, or something else, but my parents are incredibly strict and overprotective. I'm not allowed to do anything my friends get to do. R-rated movies, getting rides from older kids, staying out late on school nights? Forget it. The weird thing is, my dad was a total hippie when he was a teenager. His parents had no control over him whatsoever. He played drums in a rock band and supposedly had gigs all over the state. Once in a while he slips up and tells some story about how he hitchhiked hundreds of miles to go to a concert, or skipped school to go to a Vietnam War protest—but then he gives me some big, stern lecture about how times were different then, and my job is to stay in school and keep out of trouble.

Dad and Mom are both high-school teachers now—he teaches history and she does music—so it seems to me that they survived their crazy hippie teen years in one piece. And if it was good enough for them, why was I supposed to sit in my room alone every Friday and Saturday night playing video games? And not even the fun, Mature-rated ones where you get to blow people up and stuff? But there was no way on earth they were going to let me go to a protest. And especially not a protest with Courtney. Even though, like I said, they might have been rebels in their day, my parents are horrified by Courtney. I think she's incredibly hot, but she's hot in a Gothy way that apparently threatens the senior-citizen crowd. She wears lots of black eyeliner, dyes her hair lots of crazy colors, and is pretty pierced up. The first time my mom saw Courtney, she asked me, "Why would a girl need five piercings?" Meanwhile, I was thinking, *Oh, you mean five piercings you can see?*

Dad calls Courtney "Vampirella." I'm pretty sure that's not a compliment.

So I lied to my parents. I took my beautiful Martin acoustic guitar and left. I told them I was walking over to my drummer Tim's house to work out some songs, when really I was going to Courtney's, and then from there to City Hall. I wasn't even sure exactly what the protest was for. Courtney was kind of an activist, so she was always protesting against something: income inequality, or one of America's wars, or some huge corporation that was raping the environment. I could barely keep track of the news, partly because I spent every spare moment of my life practicing my guitar, or writing songs, or reading about music. Courtney got mad at me sometimes. In fact, she said she wasn't sure she could ever go out with me seriously until I became a "serious person"—whatever that is. She said I didn't care about anything, which wasn't true at all. I just felt powerless to change anything. I mean, give me a break. First of all, I had spent my whole life protesting against my parents' insane rules and regulations, but I still wasn't even allowed to chew gum in my house (don't even ask)—so I knew firsthand that protesting didn't always change the world. Besides, I also knew that my dad had spent his teen years marching on Washington, and the next four decades bitching about how useless it had all been.

But music was something else. When I was playing an electric guitar plugged into a huge amplifier, the sound waves didn't have to stop a war, or save a whale, or teach an Eskimo to recycle—they didn't have to do anything but move the air around me. That was enough. The music pushed everything else away.

Plus, girls extremely loved it when I played guitar for them. Extremely.

Yeah. Anyway. I got to Courtney's house around eight. She answered the door and I forgot to breathe for a few seconds. She was wearing all black, as usual, but she was wearing a lot of layers of tight, sparkly, shiny black with rips and slits in it, so there was skin flashing everywhere. I had a feeling her parents weren't around, because she grabbed the front of my jacket, yanked me into the house, and said, "Thanks so much for doing this, Rich! You're the best!" Then she put her free hand on the back of my neck and kissed me so hard I felt her nose ring mash into my face.

I'm telling you, it's the guitars.

Eventually, we walked the few blocks down to the protest scene. She was in a hyper mood, and kept up a constant stream of commentary about whatever cause this protest was about. Unfortunately, I was feeling equally hyper about my performance, and I was also hormonally distracted, so I didn't do much listening. I heard little snippets, like, "Why should these poor people be in such pain when . . ." and "This has already been legal in California for years . . ." I tuned it all out, because my thoughts just kept flashing between three completely different channels:

1. Mom and Dad Better Not Call Tim's House
2. Did I Remember to Bring My Guitar Picks? My Tuner? My Capo? Will I Panic and Forget the Songs? Will I Break a String?
3. Should We Just Go Back to Courtney's House and Make Out Some More?

Downtown, Courtney took my free hand and pulled me into a big tent that had been set up in the plaza in front of City Hall. There were police all around the outside of the tent, but inside there were just lots and lots of grungy-looking people who looked like they had been sleeping in there for days without taking breaks for hygiene. There was kind of a funky odor in there, too—a weird mix of body odor and something that was almost-but-not-quite cigarette smoke—but I was still too stoked up from Courtney's kiss and the excitement of skipping out on my parents to mind. Courtney never really seemed fully alive at school, but in this tent she was sparking like a jumper cable, practically skipping all over to introduce me to a whole network of older teenagers and even adults. She knew everybody, and everybody knew her. Courtney was a big shot here.

Our little "Tour de Tent" ended at a raised platform that held a stool and a microphone. Above it hung a banner proclaiming THE SUFFERING ENDS NOW! I still had no clue what the cause was supposed to be, but ending the suffering now sounded like an idea I could get behind. Courtney tapped the shoulder of a huge, hairy old hippie guy with a beard you could have hidden a treehouse in, and he nodded when he saw my guitar case. "Hey, man," he said to me, "it's great to see the young people supporting the cause. These people have been down here all day working to get our message out. Are you ready to rally their spirits?"

"Uh, sure," I said.

"Then let's stick it to the man!"

Whatever that means, I thought.

He led me to the stage, leaned way down so that his mouth was only a foot or so higher than the mic, and boomed out, "YOUR ENTERTAINMENT IS HERE!" When

the screeching burst of feedback triggered by his enthu-
siasm subsided, he continued: "So, uh, let's have a warm,
herbal welcome for my good friend"—he paused and looked
at Courtney, who mouthed my name—"RICH!"

I jumped up onto the platform while half the people
clapped politely and the other half winced at the second
piercing wail of feedback. I took my guitar out of its case,
checked my tuning as fast as I could, took a deep breath of
the smoky, musty air, and started playing the best protest
song I knew: Bob Dylan's "I Shall Be Released." I thought
my voice sounded pretty good, and I was nailing the guitar
part. I mean, I knew 1960s music the way a lot of guys my
age knew sports statistics. I studied it. I sweated it. I lived
it. I could play Bob Dylan songs as easily as the jocks at my
school could throw a lateral pass (whatever that was). In
a strange way, I had always felt that I should have been a
teenager in the '60s, when guitarists were at the center of
rock music, and rock music was at the center of the world.

Unfortunately, when I looked up, the crowd wasn't exactly going nuts. Some people were into what I was doing,
and others were at least kind of checking me out, but a
lot of people, especially toward the back of the tent, were
chatting with the people around them. Then I noticed that
there was even one old, sick lady in a wheelchair pulled up
near the corner of the platform off to my right. She had an
IV tube in one arm and an oxygen mask over her mouth.

I thought, *What kind of protest is this, exactly? That lady should be in a hospital, not under a smoke-filled tent.*

I finished that song, and most people clapped, but it wasn't like the crowd went wild or anything. I was sort of embarrassed. Courtney was there. I had to do better. I racked my brain for a protest song that might get the people more involved, and realized it would have been a great idea if I had paid attention when Courtney was telling me about the event. Now if I asked her what kind of protest this was, she would think I was the biggest idiot ever.

There was only one thing to do: keep playing. I busted out with another big song: a civil rights anthem called "We Shall Overcome." I wasn't expecting the whole tent to break into a gigantic sing-along or anything, but the response was still exceptionally dead. Dead? That gave me a genius idea. When the song ended, I beckoned Courtney over, and asked her to go to the sick lady to see whether she had any requests. I almost said "last requests," but caught myself.

While I was waiting for Courtney to come back, I played a John Lennon song called "Give Peace a Chance." Even a freaking Beatle didn't get much of a reaction. Despite the coolness of the fall night, huge droplets of flop-sweat began forming on my forehead. If you can't get a liberal hippie protest crowd going with the Beatles, you might as well just hang it up.

Courtney came to the edge of the platform, leaned down, and whispered in my ear, "Her name is Emmy, and she wants you to play Rainy Woman Something Something? I don't know, it was hard to hear her. She can't really talk very well. But it was definitely about Rainy and a Woman. Oh, and she said something about Bob Dylan?"

Wow, I actually knew what song she meant. It wasn't a protest song, though. It was called "Rainy Day Women #12 & 35," but the title doesn't have much to do with the lyrics. In terms of what the song is actually about, let me just say most people think it's called "Everybody Must Get Stoned." I knew how to play it, although I wasn't allowed to play it at home. My parents were gigantic Bob Dylan fans just like I was, but they were also crusading anti-drug and -alcohol fanatics. They almost never talked about it in front of me, but I had caught enough slips of conversation over the years to know the basics of the situation. My dad's father, who died when I was a baby, was apparently a raging alcoholic. In case that weren't bad enough, my dad had had an older brother named Michael who died at age eighteen of a heroin overdose. Michael's name was almost never spoken aloud, but I knew a few things about him. I knew I had inherited his lefthandedness, his guitar talent, and his jet-black hair. I also knew he had died in the fall sometime, because every year there was always one week when my dad would get even more strict, quiet, and morose than usual. Then one night, Dad would lock himself in his basement office for hours and listen to 1960s music until way, way into the middle of the night. His mood would gradually return to what passed for normal afterward, and we would sort of agree to forget to say anything about Dad's long-lost sibling for another year.

So, yeah. I knew the song, and had played through it a couple of times. There were two reasons why it seemed like an odd choice for me to play, though. First of all, it had a huge harmonica part, and I didn't have a harmonica. I thought really fast, and decided I could probably fake my way through by whistling it. Second of all, though, the song wasn't about protesting at all. It was about getting high. But I looked at Courtney, who was looking at me the way a girl looks at a boy when she thinks he's about to do something really nice for an old lady in an oxygen mask. Then I looked at the old lady, who looked at me like she was an old lady in an oxygen mask. I sighed. *Well,* I thought, *it's not like anybody's really listening anyway.*

Turns out I was wrong about that part.

I cleared my throat and said, "The next thing I'm going to play for you isn't what you would call a traditional protest song. It's a special request for a lovely lady over here named Emmy. Can we please give her a big hand?"

I gestured in Emmy's direction, but I didn't have to. She was a popular figure in that tent. If there had been any seats, I was pretty sure the very mention of Emmy's name would have gotten a standing ovation. As it was, she got some serious rocking applause. Then everybody turned to me. Now I actually had the undivided attention of the entire audience. In fact, the sudden burst of approval had been so loud that the police outside had even edged their way under the flaps all around. So had dozens of little boys in—oh, God—Cub Scout uniforms. What was that about?

I gulped. I hoped the cops were Bob Dylan fans. I strummed the first chord of the song, and started whistling the harmonica part, just as one more person pushed his way through the Scouts in the back of the tent: my father.

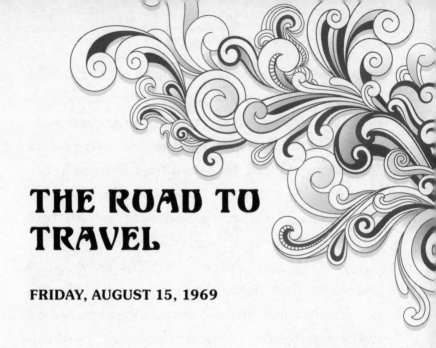

THE ROAD TO TRAVEL

FRIDAY, AUGUST 15, 1969

I stared at the girl. "Nineteen sixty-nine? Woodstock?"

She nodded. I felt faint. This wasn't possible. It really, really wasn't. Although it did explain the new-old cars. The clothes. The lack of cell phones. "Did you hit your head when you fell?" she asked.

I rubbed all around my skull, very gingerly. Nothing hurt. In fact, aside from my throbbing hip, I felt pretty good for a kid who'd just flown back through forty-five years of time and then gotten T-boned by a Cadillac. "No," I said. "Uh, why did you say I was all white like an angel?"

"Because you are!" she said. She reached for my hair again, and pulled a lock down in front of my right eye. It was white. Shiny, satiny white. "Michael, David," she called, "come here! And can you bring some clothes for the angel here to put on? It's all right, Michael, I don't think you killed him!" As her friends detached themselves from the side of their car, she said, "I'm Willow. Do you have a name? If you're on the run from the heat or something, you can just tell me a name to call you. Nobody's going to hassle you, man."

I thought about it. I had seen way too many movies about people from the future messing up the past, so even in my state of blinding panic I knew I shouldn't use my real first name. "You can just call me . . . Gabriel."

Willow grinned. "That's groovy, man," she said. "Like the angel Gabriel, right?"

Actually, Gabriel is my real middle name, but when a beautiful girl thinks you've done something groovy, you go with it. I just smiled in what I hoped was a mysterious manner. Just then, the two guys crouched down beside the ditch. The younger one put a paper bag on the ground next to me and mumbled, "Clothes." He didn't look me in the eye. I guessed he felt guilty about his friend running me over.

The older one locked his gaze right onto mine and said, "Hi. I'm Michael, and this is my little brother, David. You've already met my old lady, Willow. Are you all right, man? I'm really sorry about this whole scene. I don't know what happened. . . . One minute, the road was clear. The next, WHAM! Anyway, you okay?"

I told him I was.

His smile was as warm as Willow's. "That's great news! I didn't know what we were going to do if we had to call the fuzz, man. I mean, what if they wanted to, like, look in the trunk or something?"

I didn't understand, so I just looked at him blankly.

Willow leaned down and whispered in my ear: "We're holding, man."

Holding what? I wondered. Then it dawned on me. I had read a ton of books and articles about Woodstock, plus I had seen the famous documentary movie, and they must have been holding the same stuff in their car that hundreds of thousands of other people had brought to the concert: drugs.

I was still completely naked, and although the crowd had dissipated once it became apparent I wasn't dying or anything exciting like that, I actually felt more embarrassed in front of three people whose names I now knew than I had in front of a couple dozen strangers. "Um, could you all maybe turn around for a minute or something so I can put on whatever's in this bag?"

Michael and David retreated to the car, and Willow just stood at the edge of the ditch with her back to me. I looked into the bag, which contained a tie-dyed T-shirt, underwear, blue jeans, and a beat-up pair of Keds sneakers. I put the shirt on first, because there was no way to stop hugging my knees without exposing myself to two lanes of slow-moving hippie traffic until I had that on. It fit perfectly. Then I got the underwear on with as little uncurling of my legs as possible, and finally, I lay back in the ditch and wriggled into the jeans, which also fit me. I gasped when they touched my injured hip, though. I twisted around to look at the damage for the first time, and saw that I had been branded by the Cadillac's hood ornament, so that my skin was bruised in the shape of a broad V with a fancy shield in its center.

I buttoned up the pants and did my best to stand. My right leg buckled under me and I almost fell, but Willow whirled around and caught me. "Michael, David, help me!" she said. "Gabriel can't walk by himself."

Michael sprinted the few steps over and put his shoulder under mine. His brother just stood next to the car, paralyzed. Willow's eyes flashed as she barked at him, "Get over here!"

As David finally stepped toward us, I got my first really good look at his face. Even though Willow and Michael were both pretty strong, I almost fell over again. Willow said, "David James Barber, sometimes I just don't know where your mind goes."

My knees went. David James Barber was my father.

The three of them got me into the backseat of the car, where I proceeded to give in to a massive case of the shakes. David—Dad—got in right next to me, while Michael ran around to the driver's side and fired up the engine, and Willow threw herself into the passenger seat. "Come on, Michael," she said. "We have to get to the festival. Maybe there'll be a doctor there or something. I think Gabriel might be in shock."

In shock, I thought. *Why would I be in shock? It's thirty years before I was born, and I'm sitting next to my fifteen-year-old dad, in a car full of illegal drugs. Oh, and the driver is my dead uncle. Who just ran me over. Stop me when we get to the shocking part.*

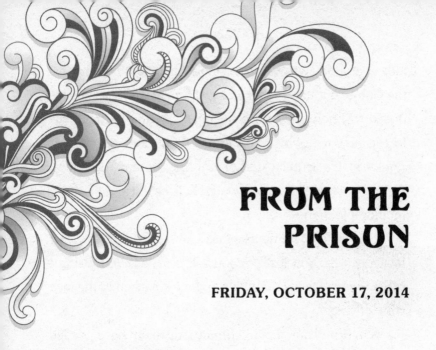

FROM THE PRISON

FRIDAY, OCTOBER 17, 2014

"What were you thinking?" my dad thundered at me, as he held an ice pack to his swelling left eye. Like he really had to raise his voice to be heard from half a foot away in our five-foot-wide cement holding cell.

"I don't know," I mumbled, my head in my hands.

"Lying to your parents? Sneaking to your girlfriend's house? Leading a sing-along of 'Everybody Must Get Stoned' at a medical marijuana legalization rally? In front of dozens of police officers . . . AND five busloads of Cub Scouts?"

"Um, technically, the song is called 'Rainy Day Women #12 & 35.' Plus, I didn't exactly know what the rally was for. Courtney just told me it was a protest. And I had no idea everybody was going to sing along like that. Oh, and the Cub Scout thing—that was just freaky. How was I supposed to know they were having their annual field trip to the mayor's office? You know, if you look at this the right way, it's actually kind of amusing. I mean, don't you think the whole adventure made their field trip a lot more memorable than—"

"This is NOT funny, Richard Gabriel Barber. You just incited a riot. You just got yourself arrested. You just got ME arrested. Dammit, you just got me smacked in the face with a flying IV pole."

As it turned out, that old Emmy lady might have needed an oxygen mask and a wheelchair, but she still had plenty of fight left in her. When the Cub Scouts had started to join in with the sing-along, which admittedly was a horrifying moment, the mayor had appeared and ordered the police to turn off my microphone. But when the first officer got within five feet of the stage, Emmy went berserk, wheeled her way over to me faster than I would have thought possible, grabbed the mic pole, bent it down into her face, shouted, "MARIJUANA FOREVER," and started swinging it in all directions. I just sat on my stool, not knowing what to do, as my father came barreling toward me through the suddenly milling mass of charging police, angry protesters, and screaming Scouts. By the time he reached the stage, there were five officers doing battle with Emmy and the huge bear-man who had introduced me. Emmy had lost her mic stand and had switched weapons. When her IV pole caught Dad's forehead, I tried to jump off the stage to drag him away from the center of the storm. Unfortunately, one of the officers saw me stage-diving, grabbed my arm, and cuffed me to Dad.

So, an hour or so later, here we were.

Courtney walked past the bars of our cell, escorted by a female officer. She looked delighted. "My mom's here to get me. They're letting me off with a warning. Call me, okay? 'Everybody Must Get Stoned'—that was badass! You're a legend! Sorry 'bout your eye, Mr. B.!"

Dad subjected me to what might have been the most disapproving look I had ever received from him. "I hope you got a nice last look at her, Rich," he said. "Because you won't be seeing her again outside of school for a lo-o-ong time."

"What are you talking about?"

"What am I talking about? I'm saying you're not going to be allowed to see your girlfriend again until I say so."

"Why? This wasn't her fault. It was mine."

"Did she ask you to play at that protest?"

"Yes, but—"

"Did she ask you to break your parents' rules and come over?"

"Yes, but—"

"Did she—"

"DAD! Stop! I decided to play at the protest, all right? Courtney asked me to, but I decided. And Courtney didn't tell me to lie to you. She didn't even know I lied. She just asked me over, and I lied so that I could make it happen."

My father smiled evilly. I hadn't even known he knew how to smile evilly. What a little learning adventure we were having. "Well, this is perfect, then. Because I'm not grounding Courtney. I'm grounding you. And to think, kids say parents don't know how to be fair."

I sat and fumed for a while. There's nothing worse than evil dad humor. "Um, Dad?" I said. "You know, you played at protests when you were a teenager."

"Yes, Richard, but I always knew what they were for."

"You never let me do anything. I had to sneak out. Your parents let you travel hundreds of miles to go to concerts."

Dad leaned toward me and said, "My parents didn't care where I was." Too late, I realized he was actually furious; now every time he said something, I could feel a slight spray of spit.

"I've never been anywhere. You went to freaking Woodstock!"

Dad did something then that he had never done before. He dropped his ice pack and grabbed my jaw, hard. Then he hissed in my face, "My brother *died* because of Woodstock."

Dad always did have a knack for the conversation-killing one-liner. After that, we sat and stared at the rusting bars, listening to our own breathing and the random noises of the people in all the other cells for what felt like days, until finally a guard came and got us. My mother was waiting with my guitar case just beyond the thick, dead-bolted door that led out of the holding area, but she wasn't allowed to take us home until Dad signed a whole bunch of papers at a desk and listened to a long lecture. This didn't help his mood.

It was almost midnight by the time Mom got to hug and kiss Dad. I tried to hug her, too, but at first, it was like hugging a tree trunk. Then she wrapped her arms around me so hard I thought my ribs would give in, and started crying in my hair. Then she choked and stuttered into my ear, "H-how . . . cou-could you . . . be . . . s-so st-stupid?"

I think it's safe to say we all had a long ride home.

The instant we entered the house, I got sent straight to my room. There was no "Thank goodness you're all right" or "We love you even though you made a mistake." In fact, the only thing that came out of either parent's mouth was a hearty "We'll discuss your punishment for this fiasco tomorrow" from Mom.

I got ready for bed, and tried to go to sleep, but my mind was racing about a million miles an hour. I kept picturing Courtney grabbing my head and kissing me . . . the cop grabbing my arm and cuffing me . . . my father grabbing my jaw and hissing in my face. It had been quite the grabby evening. Plus, there was the crowd singing along with my words as the police moved in on the stage. Obviously, it hadn't worked out terrifically well, but the moment had been kind of awesome.

And then there were the last words my dad had said to me all evening: "My brother died because of Woodstock." I didn't know what that was about. I knew my uncle hadn't actually died *at* Woodstock, or Dad never would have mentioned the concert weekend at all, just like he never mentioned anything about where or when, exactly, his brother's death occurred, and never said a word about the funeral.

I thought I knew a lot about Woodstock, especially compared to a lot of kids my age, who didn't know much about the sixties, except maybe that there used to be some people called hippies. I had seen the documentary film a million times, mostly so I could try to copy the guitar solos of the amazing people who had played there, like Carlos Santana and Jimi Hendrix. I had picked up most of the other basic info between guitar solos, too: Woodstock was a massive concert in Upstate New York. It took place over three days in August 1969, in a farmer's field, and 500,000 people came. There were gigantic traffic jams for miles and miles around on the way into the concert site, and a lot of the bands had to be flown in by helicopter. The organizers only expected maybe 100,000 people to show up, so there were shortages of food, medical supplies, toilets, parking, and just about everything else you can think of. Also, the weekend featured tremendous rainstorms that turned the entire area into a mess of deep, reeking mud. There were drugs everywhere. Hundreds of people went skinny-dipping in a lake a few hundred feet down a hill behind the stage. Babies were born. A couple of people died.

But—and this was the amazing thing that my dad had once talked about glowingly to me—there were no riots. There was no looting. People shared whatever food and supplies they had. Over the entire course of the weekend, half a million young people lived together in these primitive, crowded conditions without a single injury due to fighting. Everybody got along. The hippie generation proved to the world that they could live their ideals of peace and love, at least for a while.

Then my dad came home, experienced the death of his brother, and grew into a bitter old man who thought the right way to raise a kid was to keep him locked in a room until college.

Usually when I had a truly raging case of insomnia, I would text Courtney. She always put her phone on mute before bed, so she never texted back in the middle of the night, but at least it let me feel like I wasn't completely alone. I got up, turned on my light, and looked around for my phone, but realized it was probably downstairs somewhere. My alarm clock said it was 2:23 a.m., so I figured my parents were long since asleep, and it would be safe to tiptoe past their bedroom and retrieve the phone.

I figured wrong. My mom was sitting at the kitchen table, barely illuminated by the tiny stovetop light, drinking a cup of her horrible-smelling flowery herbal tea. "You couldn't sleep either, huh?" I whispered, in a pathetic attempt to establish common ground.

"Do you know what day this was?" She said this in a stinging voice, like she was trying to cut me with the words.

I didn't say anything. All I could think of was wisecracks, and she was holding a mug of boiling liquid. It didn't seem like a great time to antagonize her.

"Your uncle Mike died on October seventeenth."

Ouch. Of all the days to get busted at a pro-drug rally . . .

"Do you know what your father does every year on October seventeenth?"

I just kept staring at her, thinking, *Still not talking . . . still not talking . . . must bite tongue . . .*

"He sits in his den in the basement all night until dawn with his brother's things . . . photos, an old guitar, an amplifier."

A guitar? An amplifier? My father had an amplifier downstairs my whole life? I have to explain: My parents had bought me a really great acoustic guitar—the beautiful Martin I had played at the protest—as soon as I had proven I was serious about playing. In fact, my dad had insisted on getting a Martin, even though Martins are expensive, because he said that a Martin was "the only serious choice" if I was going to play popular music. But when it came to electric, I had spent years begging him for an amp before he let me get the world's teeniest model, and he still made me practice through headphones whenever he was home. Whatever.

"He usually goes down there at around nine thirty or ten, but I suppose you've never noticed before. He tries really hard not to talk about it. Let me tell you a story, Richie."

Richie? She hadn't called me "Richie" in, like, seven years. It had sounded a lot nicer back then. I had the feeling this was going to be some story.

"A long time ago, there was an extremely sweet, extremely confused eighteen-year-old boy. He was talented and beautiful. Some say he looked, sounded, and even acted a lot like you. This boy had a younger brother who loved him very much. One night, when the younger brother was away from home on a high-school marching band trip, something terrible happened. The older boy locked himself in the brothers' shared bedroom at around ten thirty, sat down on his bed, tied a length of rubber tubing around his right arm just above the elbow, and stuck a needle full of an awful drug called heroin into a vein in that right arm. Then he untied the rubber tubing, pushed down on the plunger of the needle, and sent the heroin into his bloodstream."

I noticed Mom's voice was quivering. Mom's voice never quivered.

"The boy had apparently been experimenting with heroin for two months or so, but nobody really knew about it at the time. Anyway, for some unknown reason, he took too much this time. Immediately, his heart rate slowed down. His breathing became shallow and uneven. His pupils shrank to pinpoints. He became confused. He may have realized that this time he had gone too far. He may have become frightened . . . or maybe he was so far gone, so fast, that he never even knew what was happening to him. His lips and fingernails turned blue.

"Within a minute or two at most, this beautiful young man fell off his bed and landed facedown on the bare hardwood floor, breaking his nose and several of his front teeth. This must have made quite a loud noise, but his mother and father, who were drinking and watching television in another room, never heard a thing. At this point, his body probably flailed and twitched around the floor in violent convulsions for several minutes, but the parents remained unaware that their first-born child was dying alone."

Tears were running freely down Mom's face now. She wiped them with the back of one hand but never stopped telling her story.

"In fact, it wasn't until six o'clock the next morning, when the younger brother came home from his band trip, that the body was discovered. The parents woke up, still intoxicated from the night before, to find their younger son screaming hysterically. He had entered his bedroom without turning on the light because he didn't want to wake his beloved big brother—so he tripped and fell over the cold, lifeless thing on the floor."

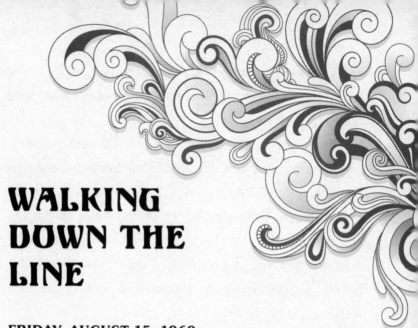

WALKING DOWN THE LINE

FRIDAY, AUGUST 15, 1969

Oh, *my God*, I thought. *My father is a demented, hyperactive maniac. With sideburns.*

Being the same age as my dad was weird enough. Watching him practically bouncing off the ceiling of the car with excitement was the one thing that almost pushed my entire time-travel experience beyond my capacity for belief. While I was leaning back against the seat, aching and shaking, my father—who was destined to spend every weekend night of his adult life sitting at the kitchen table with a crossword puzzle—was rattling on a mile a minute about the concert:

"Wow, do you think we're going to get there in time to see the first act? Are we going to get good seats? This is going to be so wild, man! Think about it. We're going to see the Who! We're going to see Janis Joplin! We're going to see Jimi Hendrix! Hey, Michael, turn up the radio! Willow, tell him to turn up the radio! Please? Oh, wow, it's the Beatles! I heard they might even show up. Do you think it's true? Huh, Mike? Do you think the Beatles might be there?"

He was like a five-year-old who really, really needed to be medicated.

I sat up to look at Michael and Willow and caught my reflection in the huge rearview mirror. Suddenly, I felt another huge wave of shock. My hair really was completely white-blond. So were my eyebrows. I looked like the illegitimate love child of my normal self and Luna Lovegood from the Harry Potter movies. What was I going to do? What if I never got back to my own time? What if my hair stayed this way? What if . . .

"TURN THIS UP!" my dad shouted, showering the side of my face with flecks of spit. *Well,* I thought, *there's one habit he never lost.* The song on the radio was called "Get Back." It was by the Beatles, and I knew it because I had taught myself the guitar parts. Willow turned it up, and Dad and Michael both started singing the vocal at the top of their lungs. Most Beatles songs have tons of vocal harmonies, but there aren't any harmony parts in most of that one. Still, I'm good at singing harmony, because that was pretty much the one part of my musical career my mom, the music teacher, found interesting, so when the song got to the chorus, I joined in with a high harmony part. Willow looked around from Michael to Dad to me with a huge, beautiful smile on her face as we sang,

Get back to where you once belonged.

My father and my uncle sounded so perfectly at ease together that you could just tell they did this all the time, and Dad looked so happy, it barely seemed possible he could grow into the man who had raised me. As for me, when my voice blended with theirs, I almost stopped singing. We sounded amazing. We sounded like we belonged together. We sounded like a family. I didn't want the song to end.

I knew the next song, too. It was "Everyday People" by Sly and the Family Stone, who would be playing at Woodstock. They had male and female singers, and Willow belted out the female parts while the three of us did all the guy harmonies. Willow banged her hand on the dashboard like she was playing a cowbell, I hummed the bass part whenever I didn't have a singing part, and Dad rocked forward and back so hard the entire car shook. His hair flew all over the place. It hit me that my father had really, really long, wild hair—hippie hair. *Dude,* I thought, *your students would freak if they could see this.*

Dad, Michael, and Willow sang maybe ten more songs,

some of which I knew, and some of which I had never heard in my life. Apparently, the number-one song in the entire country the week of Woodstock was something called "In the Year 2525" by Zager and Evans. I sang along with the choruses of most of the songs I hadn't heard, but this was so strange I had to listen. I mean, here was a song about the future . . . and I was actually a kid from the future. I could feel the newly blond hair stand up all along the backs of my arms and the nape of my neck. Willow noticed I had gotten quiet, and stopped singing. "What's wrong?" she asked. "You were looking so much better for a while."

"Nothing," I said. "I just don't know this song."

She laughed her tinkly laugh. "You must have amnesia, Gabriel. This song is everywhere! It's so far out!" Then she stopped smiling as she looked around and noticed we weren't moving. "Gee, how much farther, Mikey?" she asked. "We still need to get Gabriel checked out."

The traffic had been getting slower and slower ever since I had gotten into the car, but now we were at a complete standstill in front of a combination gas station and general store. Lines of teenagers were walking past us on both sides of the street, carrying sleeping bags, backpacks, and a wide variety of other stuff on their backs. There were also cars pulled off and parked haphazardly everywhere. When I really stopped to think about it, I noticed that there had been more and more parked cars and teenage pedestrians for miles, but I had been so busy pretending the Barber 3 were the Jackson 5 that I hadn't thought about it. The street sign said we were at the corner of Route 17B and Route 52. Michael put the car in park (which didn't really make any practical difference in our progress) and dug out a road map. I had never seen anybody actually use one of those in a car before. I reached for my pocket to get out my cell and see where we were, and had to fish around in there for a moment before I realized my cell was in my living room, forty-five years away.

After studying the map for a couple of minutes, Michael said, "I think we're still about six miles away from the festival. But we're not moving at all. I'm going to pull over and park here. Then I think we should go into this store and buy as much food as we can eat."

"Then what?" Dad asked.

"Then, little brother, we walk."

There were cars parked two and three rows deep in a grassy area behind the store, so Michael angled the Cadillac in between a VW minibus painted up in DayGlo peace signs and a beat-up Jeep that looked like it had survived World War II. What a weird thought—this was only twenty-four years after World War II, so that was completely possible.

We went into the store, which was already nearly picked clean. A scraggly-looking old lady in overalls was scurrying around with a sticker gun, raising the prices of the remaining items. "Quick!" Michael said. "Grab a bunch of stuff that won't go bad."

I followed Dad and Willow as they went on a quick scavenger hunt through the three aisles of merchandise, snatching up a loaf of bread, a package of crackers, a jar of peanut butter, a big container of orange juice, two tins of sardines, and a few other items I didn't get a good look at. Then Willow started piling my arms high.

"Uh, just so you know, I don't have any money or anything," I said.

"We know," she replied. "I mean, like, where exactly where would you have kept your wallet?" I could feel myself blushing as she laughed and gently hip-checked me into an empty display case. "Just pay us back by being kind to somebody else in the future, okay? It's good karma!"

We went to the register to pay and found Michael already standing there with two cases of soda. He was muttering under his breath as the lady rang up the person in front of him. "Can you believe this? A dollar for a six-pack of Cokes? Seventy-five cents for a box of Corn Flakes? These people are deliberately overcharging just because they can!"

"Shh, Mikey," Willow whispered.

"No, I'm going to say something. This isn't right."

"Come on, Mike. Let it go. We don't need some big hassle before we even get to the concert. You promised you were going to make this trip perfect for your brother, right?"

"Yeah, but . . ."

She put her packages down on the floor and hugged him from behind. "No buts. You said you wanted David to remember this trip forever."

From behind, I could see Michael's entire frame tense up, then relax. "You're right," he said. "This whole scene isn't worth getting wigged out over."

Michael stepped up to the counter and paid for everything. When the lady said, "Have a nice day," he looked like he was choking on a lemon, but he didn't say a word.

I thanked my hosts profusely as we walked to the car and packed all of our groceries into the backpacks they had brought. They loaded me down with a sleeping bag and a folded-up camping tent, and we set out along the edge of the road, following the thousands of excited teen pilgrims whose ranks extended as far as I could see into the distance. My hip ached, but I distracted myself by checking out the fashion show that was going on around me. I was actually surprised by how normal a lot of people's clothing looked to me. I mean, the majority of the kids around us were sporting jeans and T-shirts. If I had seen one of them alone back in the 2010s, I wouldn't have noticed anything astounding about the outfit. But seeing a horde of them all walking at once, several things struck me. First, in my time, an army of teens heading to a summer concert would all have been wearing shorts. Second, the T-shirts didn't all have corporate logos on them—I was so used to advertising slogans and trademarks everywhere that it was sort of a shock to see nothing but plain old solid colors and stripes.

Then there were the occasional bikers roaring by every few minutes, plus the serious hippie kids like Willow, who were wearing fringed vests, love beads, tie-dyes, bandanas on their heads, and a wide variety of other eye-popping outfits. And, speaking of eye-popping, I couldn't help but notice a remarkable lack of bra-wearing among a large percentage of the female population.

Two other things shocked me. One was that almost everybody was skinny. I know my parents are always complaining about the obesity epidemic in modern America, but wow—seeing how thin everybody was in 1969 really made me understand what they have been talking about my whole life. The other was the parade of freaky hair. You might expect long hair on guys, and that parted-in-the-middle-with-two-braids style on girls. . . . I had seen enough old *Brady Bunch* episodes to expect a certain basic 1960s look. But everywhere I turned, I was seeing white kids with four-inch Afros. Nothing had prepared me for the shock of *that*.

After only a few minutes of walking in the hot morning

sun, I broke into a pretty good sweat that loosened me up and made my hip feel better. Right after that, Dad started in on his brother:

"How much farther do we have to go? We're not going to miss the first act, are we? Is anyone else thirsty? I'm thirsty. Hey, Michael, can we drink some Cokes? That way we won't have to carry 'em. I bet Gabriel would like a Coke. Mike, Gabriel looks thirsty. I think we learned in Boy Scouts that you're supposed to give lots of fluids to people after they get hit by a car."

Wow, and I thought he was annoying when he was sixty.

On the other hand, the Coke tasted amazing. I wasn't sure if I was just super-duper hot, but it honestly seemed to me like it was better than twenty-first-century Coke. Plus, I was on my way to Woodstock! I was going to see Jimi freaking Hendrix play! Additionally, walking behind Willow was a whole other level of 1960s amazingness. I took a moment to apologize in my mind to Courtney for the thoughts I was having about another woman. In my defense, though, I didn't think it counted as cheating, because Courtney wasn't even going to be born for another thirty years.

Even with the sweet, sweet soda and the sweet sweetness of my uncle's girlfriend to keep me moving, I was starting to feel kind of draggy after a couple of miles, but then, out of nowhere, something beautiful happened.

Somebody off in the distance in front of us started singing a song:

Just what makes that little old ant
Think he'll move that rubber tree plant
Anyone knows an ant, can't
Move a rubber tree plant

But he's got high hopes, he's got high hopes
He's got high apple pie, in the sky hopes

I didn't know the song, but apparently every single other person for miles in either direction did, because suddenly I was part of the world's lengthiest singalong. Each person in the huge human chain turned to the person behind and grinned.

When that song ended, there was a moment of silence, but then another song came rippling down the line:

Puff, the magic dragon lived by the sea. . . .

The singing went on for miles. After a while, we made a sharp left turn and started heading downhill on a farm road. I could smell cow manure and wet hay. Then we came over a rise and I saw a shallow valley full of people sitting around on blankets or standing in little groups talking. At the far edge of the valley I saw a line of what looked like concession stands. It was weird, because there was no stage, and most of the crowd was still walking down the road. There was also a partially built chain-link fence that looked like it was supposed to be some sort of official entrance. I knew that, at the beginning, tickets had been sold for the Woodstock festival, but then at some point, the huge crowd had just trampled the fences, and the concert had eventually been declared free for everyone. But when had that happened? My companions had tickets, but I didn't. If I got hassled, we might get separated.

When we reached the fence line, we didn't see anybody in any kind of uniform, or any turnstiles, or any other sign of officialdom, so we just did what the rest of the crowd was doing. We kept walking.

Then we came over the far edge of that valley, and saw a sight I knew would be burned into my mind forever. I was looking downhill into a natural bowl the size of several football fields in every direction. At the bottom was a big wooden stage, flanked by several super-tall lighting towers. There were also more concession stands, a line of pay phones, and a few rows of portable toilets. But what stood out—what blew my mind—was the sheer volume of humanity on display. The entire area was totally blanketed with people.

We were at Woodstock. And my uncle Mike had sixty-three days to live.

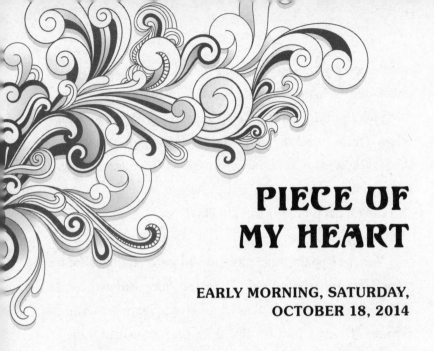

PIECE OF MY HEART

EARLY MORNING, SATURDAY, OCTOBER 18, 2014

After my mother had finished telling me her story, I asked whether I could go down to my father's den and apologize. She nodded at me ever so slightly over the lip of her teacup, and I got up and tiptoed downstairs. If I had known how many years I'd have to cross before seeing her again, I might have looked back. As it was, I just concentrated on not letting the cellar door squeak. One thing about older parents: They really hate it when doors squeak. From long years of practice, I could move around my house in the manner of a teen ninja.

I paused outside the den's door, which was closed. I put my ear right up to the wood, and when I really, really strained, I was pretty sure I could hear the faint sound of music seeping through. This was scary. First of all, my dad and I didn't do heart-to-heart talks; music was the only thing we shared. Second, we also didn't apologize to each other. Third, I had no idea what Dad was doing in there. What if he was crying or something? The idea of comforting my father was pretty ghastly.

I took a deep breath and knocked.

Nothing.

I knocked again, and this time I heard shuffling footsteps. The music stopped. Then the door opened, and there was Dad, in his dark red flannel old-guy pajamas and slippers. Behind him on the floor was a nest of stuff I hadn't seen before: photo frames, papers, old magazines and books, and even a banged-up electric guitar case. Dad sighed. "What is it, Michael?" he said. Then he caught himself, realizing he had just called me Michael. "I mean—"

"I know what you mean, Dad. I just came down to say I'm sorry. I'm sorry I lied to you and Mom, and I'm sorry I got you into a stupid situation."

Dad ran one hand through the messy gray remains of his hair. "We'll talk about this in the morning, Richard. All right?" He started to step back and swing the door shut.

"Dad, wait," I said. My heart lurched. This was not safe territory. "Mom told me what tonight was. To you, I mean. And I want to say . . . I'm sorry about that, too."

Dad stopped moving and our eyes locked.

"Dad, I can't sleep anyway. Can you . . . I mean, would you like to tell me about Uncle Michael? I'm not talking about how he died. I'm talking about who he was when he was alive."

"Rich, this isn't the time."

"There's *never* going to be a time. In my whole life, you've mentioned his name maybe five times. I've never seen a picture of him, even though people have told me I have his looks. He was one of my closest relatives, and I don't even know who he was. Tonight is the anniversary of his death, and my parents have brought him up twice. You yelled at me about him, and so did Mom. So I figure I might as well ask now, while everybody already hates me."

Dad's face contorted like he was attempting to fight off a case of demonic possession. Either that, or he was battling an incredibly strong urge to slam my head through the basement wall. He didn't battle quite hard enough. "Please just leave me alone. Go to bed."

I didn't move.

"Dad, can't you just talk to me, for once?"

"This isn't about you," he snarled.

Well, Dad, I thought, *I can snarl, too.* "You're right. Nothing's ever about me in this family. It's always about you and Mom and whatever ghosts are waltzing around in your heads. I swear to God, it's like I'm growing up in a haunted house!"

"Ghosts? *Ghosts?* How *dare* you, Richard? How dare you talk about ghosts, when my brother died forty-five years ago today?"

"Yeah, Dad. Your brother died forty-five years ago—but *you* didn't! You just *act* like you're dead already!"

My father didn't answer; he just lunged toward me and raised his hand like he was going to smack me across the face. I braced myself, and felt my heart skip. But the blow never came. Instead, Dad slammed the door in my face. My eyes burned; I told myself it was just from being awake for so many hours straight. "Nothing like a little late-night male bonding," I muttered, trudging away across the basement, into my dank little guitar practice room in the corner behind the boiler. I had spent half of the summer before freshman year soundproofing the walls with foam spray and egg cartons. I kept my classical guitar down there. The sound baffling wasn't super-effective, but it was good enough that I could do some quiet fingerpicking until I calmed down without my parents smashing in the door.

It took a lot of songs, but eventually my hands stopped shaking and I felt the anger ebbing out of me. By then, it had to be something like four in the morning, and I figured my father had to have gone upstairs to bed. No matter how temporarily relaxed I might have been feeling, I absolutely didn't want to run into him again.

I packed up my guitar, eased my practice room door

open, and peeked around the edge across the open floor of the cellar. The coast appeared to be clear. I had to go directly past Dad's den to get to the stairs, though, and the door was ajar, which was extremely unusual. Light poured from the doorway, but no shadows were moving around in there. I tiptoed across the floor until I could see in.

I realized I was holding my breath. Yes, my father was that scary. He may never have hit me, but coldness and distance can be pretty hard in their own way. I forced myself to exhale slowly, and inhale as quietly as I had ever done anything, and then look all around the den.

No Dad.

But I did see something I had never seen before. In the far left corner of the room, a closet door that had always been closed and locked was wide open. Obviously, I should have just kept walking. I know that. I've downloaded enough horror movies after my parents were asleep to know that nothing good could possibly come of this scene.

On the other hand, I wanted to know about that guitar case . . . which was still right there in the middle of the floor, surrounded by Dad's piles of mementoes . . . all the buried treasures he had never shown me in my fifteen years of living with him. Plus, I was mad enough at my father that consequences weren't way up at the forefront of my mind. AND—speaking of hidden treasures—I was dying to see that amplifier my mom had mentioned.

There was one other factor at work: Dad never, ever stayed up this late. He hadn't even made it until midnight on New Year's Eve for as long as I could remember, so it seemed to me he had to be down for the count. So I figured it was a once-in-a-lifetime chance to check out Dad's secrets.

I was too right.

The piled-up stuff was set in a semicircle, so that a person sitting on the floor could reach out and grab all of it without having to move much. I set myself down carefully in the middle, and reached for a photo album. It was dated SUMMER 1969 in stick-on DayGlo letters.

The pictures inside were all captioned in my father's handwriting, and mostly showed him and my uncle mowing lawns together, goofing around by a pool, and playing onstage in a band. There was one picture that really struck me: Dad was standing between his brother and an amazing-looking teenage girl, both of whom had their arms around his shoulders. The caption read, "With 'Mom' Willow and 'Daddy' Mike." That made me realize that the only photo of my actual grandparents in the entire book was one slightly out-of-focus snapshot of them sitting in ugly chairs, watching TV and holding cans of beer.

My dad was incredibly skinny, and looked astonishingly young. My uncle looked almost exactly like an older version of me.

After that picture came an entire page with nothing on it except for three tickets to Woodstock. My heart jumped. There were only a few more pages left in the book, and I was almost afraid to turn them. It felt like I was counting down to the end of my uncle's life.

Actually, there was only one photo left. The rest of the book was blank. That one picture was shocking enough, though. It featured Willow and my father standing slightly off to one side of the frame, while a man whose face I knew handed an electric guitar to Michael.

This was absolutely impossible!

The guitar case was right there on the floor next to me. Half of me was almost laughing at the other half for even thinking what I was thinking. There was just no way. But the night couldn't get much weirder, so I popped the latches on the case and swung open the lid to reveal an electric guitar with a sheet of looseleaf paper threaded through the strings. I stood, unsteadily, and peered at the guitar. It was an off-white Fender Stratocaster with a white pickguard. A right-handed Fender Stratocaster, strung upside down so that it could be played by a lefty. There was a pick tucked in behind the top edge of the pickguard. My knees buckled.

It couldn't be. I had seen a guitar that looked exactly like this one on the covers of several guitar magazines, and in a bunch of books, too. I had watched close-ups of that guitar being played onstage. At Woodstock. By Jimi Hendrix, the greatest rock guitarist who ever lived. My musical idol. I had done a huge biography project on him for school. I had read tons of books and magazine articles about his career, watched video clips of practically every interview he had ever done, and of course, studied his music with a burning intensity. I knew everything about his life—well, except the part where apparently he gave my uncle his most famous instrument. Forget about digging up regular, ordinary buried treasure: this was like finding out I had spent my entire life in a house that held the Holy Grail in its basement.

Except for one problem. This couldn't be Jimi Hendrix's Woodstock guitar. I knew that guitar was supposed to be in a museum in Seattle. The owners only took it out for super-special occasions, because it was worth millions of dollars.

I looked at the paper between the strings. It read,

Hold this for Gabriel. One day, he will come for it. Jimi said he will know what to do. DO NOT LET ANYBODY ELSE PLAY THIS GUITAR!

~M

My head was spinning. I knelt down between the guitar and the photo album. I read the caption under the photo:

"Jimi Hendrix walks off the stage at Woodstock on Monday, August 18, 1969, and gives this guitar to my brother, Michael Barber."

I guessed that Michael had written the note, but who in the world was Gabriel? Why was my father, of all people, holding what may very well have been the single most valuable electric guitar on the planet? I turned the note over and saw there was writing on the back, as well, in a different, spidery hand:

Gabriel, play my chord for an electric three-day pass.
                                                    ~ JMH

What was an "electric three-day pass"? A three-day pass to what? And what was "my chord"? Had Jimi Hendrix written that? I knew his middle name was Marshall, so the initials were right. And if it had been written by Jimi, I had an idea what chord he might have meant. There's this one special chord that guitarists call "The Hendrix Chord." It's called an "E-seven-sharp-nine" chord. He used it in his most famous song, "Purple Haze," and in another one called "Foxy Lady." That had to be what he was talking about.

This is where I really went off the deep end. But honestly, once you've already gotten your dad beaten up and arrested, plus he's refused your apology, and when your parents have never let you do anything even before that, how much more trouble can you possibly get in? What were they going to do—revoke my internal organs? Ground me from oxygen?

Very carefully, I took the guitar out of the case, grabbed the pick, and started tuning. The strings were way, way out of whack after the instrument had sat in its case in a basement all this time. When everything sounded right in standard tuning, I played the chord, but it didn't sound quite like the way it did when Jim Hendrix played "Purple Haze." That was when it hit me: Jimi hadn't tuned his guitar the standard way. He had always tuned all six of his strings down a half-step, so that every chord he played came out a half-step flat.

Quickly, I tuned each string down a half-step. My hands were sweating, and a little shaky. I couldn't believe I was really playing Jimi Hendrix's Woodstock Strat! I hit the chord again, and now that the guitar was in Jimi's real tuning, I could swear I felt some kind of magic *zing!* emanating through the strings and into my body. It wasn't like any feeling I had ever felt before, but it was amazing. It was almost as though I were onstage at Woodstock. I could only imagine how amazing the guitar would sound through an amplifier.

An amplifier! Mom had said Dad had one down here. With extreme caution—if all of this was true, I was wearing a two-million-dollar guitar on a forty-five-year-old strap— I walked over to the open door of my father's formerly always-locked closet. Sure enough, there was a gigantic amp in there. It was a Marshall half-stack, just like the ones Jimi Hendrix had famously used. A piece of faded, peeling masking tape on the front top edge read PROPERTY OF MICHAEL BARBER. An instrument cable was sitting on top of the amplifier, just waiting to be used. There was an outlet next to the amp, and I could see that the cord was even plugged in.

A chill ran through me. Had my father left this setup here for forty-five years, just so it would be ready for this mysterious Gabriel? If so, where was he? Why hadn't he ever shown up? Had he somehow died like Michael?

I didn't want to think these creepy thoughts anymore, alone in a basement at 4:30 a.m. with a dead man's guitar around my neck. I knew my parents usually woke up at around 5:30, so I didn't have such a huge amount of time left to put all this stuff back in order and sneak upstairs. Still, it seemed like it wouldn't hurt to just plug the guitar into the amp, turn on the power, and pretend for a minute, as long as I didn't actually play.

So, of course, my father chose that one day of his life to wake up an hour early and barge in just as I was hitting my best Hendrix pose.

"NOOOOO!!!!!!" he screamed. He didn't even sound furious. Truthfully, at first, he sounded more scared than anything else. "Richard, you don't understand what you're doing!"

"Dad, I'm holding a guitar and pretending to play an E-seven-sharp-nine chord."

"Richie, please. Listen to me. I know I was harsh before, all right? Let's just put down the guitar, and we can talk."

I thought, *Oh, now you want to talk? Sure, now that I found your top-secret priceless Jimi Hendrix guitar and massive amp in a freaking hidden basement bunker!*

"Dad, I wanted to talk last night, when I tried to apologize and you slammed the door in my face. But now . . ."

Dad looked kind of green and sick. "Now?" he asked.

"Now I just want to play!" I reached behind me and cranked the volume knob on the amplifier as high as it would go. Then I placed the fingers of my right hand ever so carefully in the correct positions on the fretboard of the guitar, smiled at my father, and played Jimi Hendrix's chord.

I felt electricity run up my arms and spread through my entire body, but somehow it wasn't burning me. It was filling me up. The chord got louder and louder, and the sensations got stronger and stronger. Then, when I felt I would explode, everything went white.

The next thing I knew, I was lying naked in a ditch.

I'M A STRANGER HERE

FRIDAY, AUGUST 15, 1969

Woodstock. I was in the middle of freaking Woodstock. Have you ever visited a movie set, like in Hollywood, or at Universal Studios Florida or something? Once on a school trip to New York City, I ended up with my class in the middle of the shooting for a Nike sneaker commercial in Times Square. This was like that feeling— *I'm in a movie*—but magnified a million times. I was in a movie as it was being filmed, and I was the only person out of the half million in attendance who knew the ending.

Crazy.

We found a space big enough to spread out two blankets a few hundred yards uphill from the stage. Michael said the volume of the music would be perfect there because we were right near the platform with the sound mixing board. For a guy with the problems I knew he had—for a guy who had hit me with a car that morning—he seemed to me like a born leader. I could see why Willow and my dad both looked at him like he was some kind of hero.

If he was the travel and seat master, though, there was no doubt that Willow was the food boss. The instant we sat down, she took over lunch duty. She was all like, "Your parents aren't here, so I'm going to be your road mom for the weekend." It was kind of sexist, but I was really tired and hungry, so if somebody wanted to take charge and put together a meal right at that moment, I was all for it.

Willow spread out everything we had bought at the store, along with a bunch of fresher food she must have already been carrying, like cheeses, bakery bread, cold cuts, fancy cookies, and fruit. She even had a little glass jar of mayo, plus a knife for spreading it. I hadn't eaten anything since lunch—and it was impossible to calculate how long ago that had been. Along with the shakiness I'd already been feeling, now I was practically drooling. I nearly reached out and yanked a roll right out of Willow's lap.

Michael raised an eyebrow. "Fresh bread? Bakery cookies? Fruit? Wow. Where'd this come from?"

Willow giggled. "Let's just say I don't think I can go back to work at the cafe when we go home to Pennsylvania."

Dad looked horrified. I felt half-horrified, but also

half-starved and half-in-love. Wait, I guess that should be a third for each of those. Anyway, Willow was a sexy, badass food thief. "I love you, Willow," Michael said. That made at least two of us.

"I know," she said. Then she handed each of us an open roll and started piling on the meats and cheeses. When we finished eating most of the fresh stuff, Willow packed everything else up for later, and we all lay back on the blankets. Michael asked me if I wanted to go and find a first-aid tent or something, but there was no way I could do that. I had been thinking about it: They would ask me my name, which I couldn't give them. They would want to call my parents, and I'd have to say, "Well, my mom lives in New Jersey. The call might freak her out, though, because she's four years younger than I am right now." And if they decided I needed to go to a hospital or something, I'd get separated from my dad and my uncle.

I told Michael I just needed some sleep, and closed my eyes. My mind was going a mile a minute. I started wondering why my father had never recognized me as Gabriel while I was growing up. Was it the white-blond hair? I looked completely different with it, so a few decades later, when I came along, with jet-black hair, it seemed logical that he wouldn't have made the connection. Then I thought about what would happen if and when I found a way to get back to the future after my "electric three-day pass." Would my dad recognize me as Gabriel at that point? How would he react? Would the shock drive him insane? Would he keel over with a heart attack?

I realized I was getting way ahead of myself. For now, I had to stick with my father and my uncle. I didn't know what to do, or exactly how or why I had ended up here—it's not often you find out there's a guitar in your basement that's secretly Jimi Hendrix's most famous instrument and also, apparently, a time machine. But I figured there had to be a purpose. Jimi Hendrix had left that note for Gabriel, and then Michael's last wish on earth had been for Gabriel to end up with the guitar. Michael's writing floated in front of my closed eyelids:

Hold this for Gabriel. One day, he will come for it. Jimi said he will know what to do.

A thrill shot through me as I realized something: By Monday morning, Jimi Hendrix would know us well enough that he would give Michael his Stratocaster, and trust me with some sort of guitar-related future mission. So there was part one of my job: meet Jimi Hendrix. I opened my eyes for a moment and scanned the throngs of people pouring in from every direction. I looked downhill at the stage, and noticed the high wooden fences surrounding it. I thought about the fact that Jimi Hendrix was already a legendary rock star, the closing act at the biggest concert the world had ever seen; and I was a

fifteen-year-old who technically didn't even exist yet. *Sure,*
I thought. *I don't see any possible obstacles to getting this
done.*

Then again, I told myself, I *will do this. I know I will,
because I'm pretty sure I already have.* This was really con-
fusing. But okay, assuming I was going to meet Hendrix,
what was I supposed to say or do? Here was the thing:
Jimi was going to die of a drug overdose, just like Michael,
only his was going to come in about a year, in 1970. Was
I supposed to warn Jimi about his own death? No, that
couldn't be, because how would the Jimi I was going to
meet in 1969 know I had to warn him that he would die in
1970? Plus, what rock star would believe a fifteen-year-old
kid who ran up to him and said, "Hey, a year from now,
in London, don't wash down a bunch of sleeping pills with
a bottle of red wine!"

I propped myself up on my elbows and snuck a peek at
Michael and Willow, who were lying on the blanket to my
right. She had taken off her fringed vest and pushed her
T-shirt up so that her stomach was exposed to the sun,
while he had taken his shirt off. They were basking in the
sun with their arms around each other, kissing and whispering as though they were alone in a dark room. I wondered how he could possibly go from being this in love to
killing himself with drugs in just nine weeks.

Hadn't my mom said my uncle had started using heroin

about two months before he died on October 17? And my father had said his brother had died because of Woodstock. That was my mission, then. I would stick with Michael and Dad, and make sure Michael didn't get his hands on any heroin. In the process, we would meet Jimi Hendrix, who would give us the guitar so that I could come back in time and do all this.

But that didn't make sense. Because if Michael didn't die, I would never get the guitar and I couldn't come back here to save him in the first place. But then I wouldn't need to. But, but, but.

This kind of crap happened all the time in Harry Potter movies and stuff like that, but then there was always some super-wise old warlock dude to explain how everything worked. And if things got messed up, they always got fixed by the time the credits rolled. But I didn't have a wise old mentor, or two more showings at 7:15 and 9:30. I had real life, or at least this crazy, time-hopping version of it. What if I screwed this up, and got stuck back in this time for the rest of my existence? What would happen forty-five years from now, when I was born? Would both of me explode?

Or what if I saved my uncle's life, but changed things enough for my dad so that he never met and married my mom? I pondered that for an extremely long time, and what I kept coming back to was this: What if I did? Selfishly, I had to admit I liked being alive, but I also had to admit my father had been amazingly and consistently miserable for the decades since October 18, 1969. Sure, Dad had flipped out when I said he'd been acting dead for forty-five years, but that didn't mean it wasn't true. Maybe he and my mother would both have been better off if my uncle had survived. Then my dad could have grown up to be an older version of the bouncing-off-the-walls kid who had sung along with the Beatles in the car, and my mom could have met some other, happier man. And okay, I wouldn't be me, but maybe there might be two happy kids somewhere who were each half me and knew their parents were actually joyful people.

Well, maybe I didn't know how this movie was going to end after all—or even whether I was going to be around for the last reel.

YOUNGER GENERATION

FRIDAY, AUGUST 15, 1969

I fell asleep in the sun for a while, and woke up to the sound of the first Led Zeppelin album playing over the PA system. Drowsily, I realized that these ancient songs were basically brand-new to everyone at the festival except me. Looking around, I saw that Willow and Michael had gone off somewhere. My father was sitting next to me with his arms wrapped around his knees. I decided at that moment I would start thinking of him as "David," especially because there was a chance I might change the past and he would never grow up to become my dad. Plus, if I slipped and called him "Dad," it would be pretty much the definition of awkward.

"You're awake," he said. *You're a genius,* I thought. In the future, I would have said it and caused a huge argument about my attitude that wouldn't end until my mother sent us both to separate corners of the house. I bit my lip.

When I didn't reply, he asked, "Are you feeling better? I know you said you just needed sleep, but you really went flying when the car hit you." He hurried to add, "Not that it was my brother's fault or anything. You just appeared, like, out of nowhere. What happened, anyway? How did you get here? And where did all your clothes go? Were you tripping? Did someone steal all your stuff and dump you by the side of the road?"

Incredible. My dad never asked this many questions in a row. I had once gone with him to Take Your Kid to Work Day, and what struck me most about his teaching style was that when he put a history question up on the board, he would just say, "Talk to me about this." Then he would lean on the edge of his desk and wait. But at fifteen, Dad was a motormouth.

"Um, I can't tell you what happened. All I can say is that my hip hurts, but nothing's broken, and I don't need a doctor or anything."

"Why can't you tell me? Are you in trouble? Can we help you, man?"

My dad—David—was incredibly hyper, but he had given me his spare clothes, and he looked completely sincere about helping, even though I was a total stranger who refused to tell him anything about myself. I know it sounds odd that I found this surprising, but my father was nice.

"You are helping me. You gave me food, and clothes, and a ride. You're letting me share your blanket." I sighed. "So I guess I owe you some kind of explanation, huh? Listen: I can't exactly tell you how I ended up naked in front of your car, but please believe that I wasn't doing anything wrong, and nobody did anything bad to me."

David nodded, and I continued.

"But I guess you could say I'm sort of on the run. Nobody knows exactly where I am. My parents are really strict. They barely let me cross the street by myself, so I'm pretty sure they would have three heart attacks and die if they could see me right now. I had to come here, though. I just feel like it's something I would regret forever if I didn't."

David frowned for the first time that day, and spit, "You don't know how lucky you are."

"What are you talking about?"

"My parents don't care if I'm dead or alive. Michael and Willow care about me more than they do. You know what Mom and Pop are going to spend this weekend doing? Drinking themselves under the table without worrying about whether I'm around to annoy them by trying to get them to eat, or go to their beds when they pass out in front of the TV."

I didn't know what to say, so I just sat there until things

felt really uncomfortable. Then David said, "It's even worse for Michael. Dad notices everything Michael does, but he says it's all crap. Michael practically raised me, but Dad constantly tells him he's useless around the house. Plus, Michael's, like, the most talented musician I've ever seen in my life, and Dad's always telling him he'll never be anything but a noisemaker. And if anything's broken around the house, it's automatically Michael's fault. He smacks Michael around all the time, too. I figure any day now, Michael's going to decide he's had enough and move out. Would you rather live at home and be a punching bag, or move in with Willow? Wait, don't even bother to answer that.

"So anyway, when I have kids of my own, I'm going to be like your parents. I'm going to watch my kids like a hawk. At least that way, they'll know I care about them."

Hmm, I definitely hadn't thought about it that way. It was astounding to think that my dad had been tormenting me all these years in order to show me love.

"That is, if I have kids at all. Maybe I shouldn't. Maybe I would just automatically be a monster like my dad, no matter what I say now."

"No!" I said, louder than I should have. David jumped a little. "I mean, you won't automatically be a monster. Wouldn't. You wouldn't be. Because you're thinking about it, right? So, right there, it seems to me like you're showing more effort than your dad does."

"Maybe," David said. "But my mom is a mess, too. What if I marry a monster, and ruin my kids' lives that way? Don't you ever worry about this stuff?"

"Not usually, but I'm worrying about it now."

"Seriously. How would you even know you're marrying a monster? Obviously, she wouldn't act like one while you were dating, or nobody would ever get divorced, because they'd know not to get married in the first place. When I decide on whatever woman I'm going to marry, I think I'll have to date her for, like, years before we make it official. Then maybe we'll wait another bunch of years before we have a kid, so we really know what the hell we're doing before we take a chance on ruining some innocent kid's life."

Wow, my dad had deliberately mapped out every single thing about his life that had annoyed me for fifteen years. On the other hand, if I told him not to follow his vision, it would mean I would never be born.

"I've thought about this a lot, and I'm pretty sure it's how I want my life to go. What do you think?" he asked.

"Uh, sounds like a plan," I said.

Willow and Michael came back, all pumped up with news. "This place is far out," Willow said. She gestured off to the left as we looked downhill at the stage. "See that forest over there? It's got trails, and tents everywhere, and little craft shops. Then, if you keep walking a little more, you get to a whole commune. It's groovy! They have a big kitchen, and art sculptures, and a big psychedelic bus. There's even a playground for little kids."

Michael took over without any signal, as though he and Willow didn't even need words to communicate. *Some people don't need to date for a million years to be sure they're right for each other,* I thought. I couldn't help wondering how amazing it would be to have parents who connected with each other that way. "Then we walked down the hill, and there's a helicopter pad. I bet that's where the bands are going to fly in, man!"

Willow continued, "We asked a man in a Woodstock uniform shirt when the concert was going to start, and he told us it wouldn't be too long now, so we decided we'd better head on back to our seats. Did you get a good rest, Gabriel? Are you all right now?"

"Yeah, I'm feeling much better, thanks."

"Are you sure? Are you absolutely sure?"

"Yes, honest."

"I can't wait for the first band," Michael said. "Sweetwater! You've heard of Sweetwater, right? A friend of mine saw them open for the Doors, and he told me their live sound was wild!"

"They're not playing first," I said. "Richie Havens is."

"No, the man in the uniform just told us that Sweetwater was going to be the first act, Gabriel," Willow said.

"He's wrong. Sweetwater gets stuck in traffic, but Richie

Havens flies here in a helicopter and—" I stopped in horror. I had blurted out stuff that hadn't happened yet, just to look smart in front of my uncle's girlfriend. Brilliant move. "I mean, I heard some kid walking by say that," I added, lamely.

David looked at me oddly, but didn't contradict me. Just then, the speakers roared to life, and the stage announcer said, "Let's welcome . . . Mister Richie Havens!" David's eyebrows shot up. Willow looked amused. Michael shrugged.

I have to tell you, the concert experience of 1969 was mind-blowingly different from what we are used to in our time. (I admit, I have only been allowed to go to one concert ever, and it was with my mother, but still, I have watched a million concert DVDs, and I know the drill.) There was no Jumbotron, so the performers were just teeny, tiny dots. Nobody around us in the audience was holding up a cell phone or a video camera to record what was going on or take a profile pic. Nobody was tweeting or posting a status. There were no huge corporate advertising banners in sight. As Richie Havens sang his first song, "Minstrel from Gault," the anti-Vietnam War lyrics washed over the crowd and there was nothing to distract us from the moment. We were all just right there, listening together.

It might sound corny, but there it is. I could feel the tribal power of half a million people all concentrating at once on the same one thing. Also, Richie Havens ruled. I can't imagine how brave you'd have to be to go onstage in front of 500,000 people with nothing but an acoustic guitar and your two backing musicians, and kick off the largest concert in history. This guy absolutely killed, though. Not only did he play well, but in between songs, he spoke in a warm, calm voice, the way you would talk to friends who were just hanging out in his living room. Plus, he came back for encore after encore.

Here was the most incredible thing, which I knew from reading about it in the future. His last encore, a song called "Freedom," was totally improvised. The promoters of the concert kept pushing him back onstage to play more because the next groups weren't ready yet, so when he ran out of songs, he made one up on the spot. It was probably the coolest song of his whole set, too.

Watching it happen in real time, I just kept thinking, *I don't know how anyone could possibly not understand that playing music is a mystical act.* I was going to feel that way several times during the weekend, but right then, seeing the entire crowd falling into a group trance for the first time, I knew that whatever else happened, I had to make sure I appreciated this once-outside-of-a-lifetime opportunity.

While attempting to meet Jimi Hendrix, save my uncle, and change my father's future—hopefully without ceasing to exist.

BEAUTIFUL PEOPLE

FRIDAY, AUGUST 15, 1969

The next guy to come out onstage was equally amazing, in a completely different way. He was a holy man from Sri Lanka named Swami something, and he gave an invocation. He said two remarkable things. The first was this:

"Music is a celestial sound and it is the sound that controls the whole universe, not atomic vibrations. Sound energy, sound power, is much, much greater than any other power in this world."

I was sitting there thinking, *Before today I would have thought that was just some kind of semi-random guru baloney. But one chord on an electric guitar actually teleported me, so I guess maybe this guy has a point. I wonder if he knows how right he is?*

Then he told the crowd how historically important they were:

"The entire world is going to watch this. The entire world is going to know what the American youth can do to the humanity. So, every one of you should be responsible for the success of this festival."

I turned to David to see what he thought of this, and almost passed out. He was casually holding a huge hand-rolled marijuana cigarette, and was about to take a massive drag on it. Because, you know, when the entire world is watching, it's definitely a good idea to show your responsibility by getting high in broad daylight. I wanted Michael to act like a big brother and yell at him, but all he said was, "Hurry up and take your hit, Davey. We all need to get mellow for Sweetwater!"

So yeah, apparently, "Daddy Michael" wasn't going to be fulfilling a major disciplinary function this weekend. Granted, tons of people around us were doing the same thing, or passing around bottles of alcohol, or engaging in any number of other legally dubious activities, but I was horrified. This was my dad. I couldn't believe he was eventually going to grow up and have the nerve to ground me for appearing at a rally for the legalization of pot for terminally ill cancer patients.

David inhaled a massive lungful of smoke, and held it until I thought his head would explode. Meanwhile, Willow took a dainty little puff, then leaned across and held the joint out to me. "Gabriel, I'm so sorry," she said. "Where are our manners? We haven't even offered any, um, flammable refreshments to our guest!"

"Uh, n-no thanks," I stammered. "I'm trying to cut down for, um, track season." Not that I was a runner, or in fact any type of athlete at all, but it was the first excuse that had flown out of my mouth somehow. I had no plans to try any drugs at Woodstock. I had gotten drunk a couple of times in my friends' basements and stuff, but I had never tried any kind of drugs before, and—even if I did decide to try them at some point—there was no *way* my first psychedelic experience was going to be with my own father.

"That's cool," Michael said. "More for us!"

If there's anything more depressing than being the designated driver of a picnic blanket, while your own father gets completely wasted beside you, I am unaware of that thing.

We all eventually lay back on the blankets for a while, just thinking. I was partly wondering about what the guru guy had said about the power of music, and partly trying not to freak out over the drugaholic-teen-dad issue. If the Swami did know that music had power over the universe, did that mean I wasn't the only person who had ever traveled through time by playing an instrument? I mean, it kind of made sense that I wouldn't be, when I thought about it. Jimi Hendrix had all kinds of songs about time-and-space travel, and he was just the one person whose guitar had happened to fall into my hands. There were other musicians who had been talking about this back in the 1960s, too, like a jazz guy named Sun Ra.

Maybe I wasn't even the only time traveler at the Woodstock Festival. I kind of smiled to myself. I was having some pretty trippy thoughts, considering I was the one person on the blanket who wasn't high.

When the next band, Sweetwater, came on and started tuning, David said, "If the whole world is watching us, and if music has so much power, man, do you think maybe we can really stop the war?" Then he coughed.

The cough was sort of a relief to me. Maybe it meant he wasn't as accustomed to smoking pot as he appeared to be.

Willow's voice floated up from the other side of David's body, all slow and dreamy now. "That's a groovy idea, Davey. You're a beautiful kid, you know that?"

I glanced over at David, and he was beaming from ear to ear. Okay, I knew he was under the influence and all, and there was something about Willow that would have made any fifteen-year-old guy feel good—but still, he was just soaking up that praise like the driest sponge you'll ever see. It was happy and sad at the same time.

Then Michael spoke so gruffly, I had to sit up and look to be sure he was really the person who was talking. "Never happen, David."

"Why not? Look at all these people. Look at all the love, Mikey."

"There's too much money being made, little brother. Too much money. Dow Chemical, Brown and Root, Monsanto—as long as all these huge companies are getting rich over there, who cares about a bunch of eighteen-year-olds getting their asses shot off in a rice paddy?"

"I care."

"Yeah, well, unfortunately, you're not a real close advisor of President Nixon, Davey."

David looked crushed. Willow had pumped him up, and his brother had popped him. Willow knew it, too. She put one arm around David, and poked Michael with her free hand. I saw her whispering in his ear. Even over the sounds of the band's final tuning notes, I was pretty certain I heard her hiss, "You promised!"

As Sweetwater went into their set, David pouted for a while, and Willow stood up to dance by herself. Their music had a mellow, trance-ish hippie groove with weird instruments like flute and cello along with bongos and lots of harmony vocals. I could have been pretty happy watching Willow doing her snaky gyrations all night, but after a couple of songs, Michael got up and hugged her. Between songs I heard him say, "I'm sorry," and then their dancing got increasingly close until it became disturbingly sexy to watch. I wondered whether people used the expression "Get a room!" in 1969.

David jumped up and said, "Let's get some food, Gabriel." I started to protest about my money situation, but before I could get a word out, he reached into his brother's backpack and pulled out a wad of singles. "It's on Mr. Lover over there." Then he giggled and snorted, both of which were noises I had never heard from him before.

I shrugged, stood, and followed as my father threaded his way unsteadily through the twilit hordes toward the distant promise of a snack. It looked like it might be a bit dicey staying together and finding our way back to Michael and Willow, but there was only one of me, and—not for the last time that weekend—I had to choose between my dad and my uncle. I can't say we walked in anything approaching a straight line, because we had to dodge dancers, randomly placed blankets, countless thousands of people still streaming in from every direction, and general, random crowd motion.

We ended up in line at a stand that said FOOD FOR LOVE in huge, wavering letters.

There were at least fifty people in front of us, and within seconds, the line started swallowing us up from behind, as well. I had been to a couple of sold-out major league baseball games, but I had never before felt such a sense of being pressed between so many people. In fact, just as the band onstage stopped playing for a moment, a short, pale girl behind me started to freak out about it.

"I can't take it, Debbie! They're all around me! Why do

they all keep looking at me? It's like they want my soul. Tell them. Tell them."

She was standing with a friend, and they both looked like they might be the same age as David and I were. The friend said, "Tell them what? I don't know what you mean, sweetie."

"Tell them they can't have my soul!"

Truthfully, I didn't think anybody had been paying any particular attention to this girl before she started screaming insanely, but naturally, we were looking at her now. Sweetwater had picked an unfortunate moment to take a breather.

Debbie gave David and me an imploring look and said, "Uh, you can't have my friend's soul, do you hear me? Her soul is off-limits!" Then she whispered, "Please play along, okay? Her name is Tina."

David raised his eyebrows, which gave me an odd sense of déjà vu, because it was the same exact thing he would do forty-five years later when he knew I was trying to get away with something. "Su-u-re," he said. Bending a bit so his eyes were level with Tina's, he said, "I promise I will not take Tina's soul. I will not even take Debbie's soul. I am hungry, though. That is why I am in this food line. Is it okay if I take a hot dog?"

Tina looked pretty confused by this complicated line of thought. "You don't . . . want . . . my soul?"

"Nope, pretty much just a wiener dog. With mustard. And maybe some relish. And a brownie. Do you think they might sell brownies here? I love brownies."

Tina's eyes lit up. "Me, too. I like the icing." Then she pouted. "I didn't even know demons ate regular food."

"Oh, I'm not a demon. I think the demon food lines are over on the other side, by the bathrooms. I'm just a kid from Pennsylvania. My name is David."

"Far out. I like vanilla icing. Or sparkly icing. Your friend's hair is sparkly. Can I call you David and Goliath?"

My father giggled again. This was a match made in heaven. Debbie rolled her eyes at me, and jerked her thumb in the direction of our companions. "Tina accidentally got dosed with some acid. What's your friend on?"

"Is it that obvious?"

"Oh, yeah. Tina's pretty spacey on a good day. But anybody who can relate to her right now has to be riding on a rocket ship of his own."

"Uh, well, he might have smoked a little something."

"How about you?"

"No, I'm the designated driver."

"The what?"

Oops. Apparently, that wasn't a 1960s term. "I'm staying straight to watch out for my friends."

"Me, too. So, what's your name? I assume it's not actually Goliath."

"Gabriel." Well, sort of.

"So, Gabriel, how did you and David get here? Tina and I both live in Astoria—that's in Queens—so we took a bus from New York City. It wasn't too bad, but I've been hearing nightmare stories all day from people who had to walk absolutely miles."

"Debbie, you wouldn't believe me if I told you. But hey, we're all here now, right? So, uh, is Tina going to be okay? And what did you mean, she got dosed with some acid?"

Debbie looked at me like I was the dumbest boy she'd ever met. "Where did your friend say you were from again?"

"Pennsylvania."

"And you don't know what 'dosed with acid' means? Wow, I'd better educate you before you end up walking naked down a road somewhere and get hit by a car or something! 'Acid' is LSD. You know, the drug? It makes you see pretty colors that aren't there, and hear voices, and stuff?"

"I know what acid is. I just meant, how did she accidentally get dosed with it? Don't you have to swallow a pill or something on purpose?"

"That's usually how it works, but these older guys were handing out cups of punch over by the fences on our way in, and we were thirsty, you know? So Tina took some, but this one dude gave me the creeps the way he was watching her drink it, and I said, 'Wait a second, did you put something in there?' But he just started laughing and said, 'Take it easy, baby. I'm just trying to bring a little color into your life.' I knocked the cup out of her hand, but I guess it was too late. Anyway, I heard that drinking a lot of orange juice is supposed to help a person calm down when they're on acid, so I'm hoping they might have some for sale here. But whatever you do, don't drink from any open containers that get passed around, unless you want to wind up like her." She nodded toward Tina, who was studying David's hair very intently and mumbling something about stars and flying. "At least, that's my advice."

"I'll, uh, keep that in mind. I need to take care of my friend and his brother this weekend, so I really can't afford to get all messed up on drugs. I mean, no offense to your friend or anything."

Debbie looked at Tina, who was now making David's hair flap and calling it "my free brown spirit bird," and snorted. "I'm deeply offended," she said. "How can you say my friend is 'all messed up on drugs'? You have no idea what a mess she is when she's straight! Anyway, where's your friend's brother? How old is he? Who's watching him now?"

"Well, nobody's watching him now. But—I mean—he's older than us. David and I are both fifteen, and his brother, Michael, is eighteen. He's back at our blankets with his girlfriend. I'm not babysitting him or anything. He's just kind of . . . well, I made a promise to myself that I'd look out for these guys this weekend. That's all. It probably sounds kind of stupid."

"No, actually, it sounds kind of sweet."

Just then, the audience off to our left started clapping more loudly than they had been. Sweetwater's set was over. In the lull that followed, I heard angry shouts from up ahead in the line.

"What do you mean, you're out of food?"

"No burgers left? What are we supposed to do, eat the music?"

"Let me speak to the manager!"

Debbie and I looked at each other. "Let's split," she said. "These vibes aren't going to be good for Tina."

I agreed that an angry mob was a much less fun scene than a peace-loving mob, so I tapped David on the shoulder and told him I thought we should take a little walk. "What about my brownies?" he asked.

"What about my orange orangey orange juice?" Tina chimed in.

I remembered something. "Hey, David, didn't we buy a thing of orange juice at the store today?"

He was too glazed to process that, but I was pretty sure we had, and that we hadn't drunk it during our afternoon picnic. That meant it had been in the August heat for half a day, but I didn't think OJ went bad the way milk did. "Debbie," I said, "if you'll follow us, we have some orange juice in our backpacks."

"I don't know," she said. "We had a pretty bad experience with the last man who offered us a free drink."

"Don't worry," I said. "I'm planning to charge you for it."

She laughed. As the shouting built in volume behind us, we began to wend our way through the dusk back toward the blankets.

AMERICA

FRIDAY, AUGUST 15, 1969

I f you've never tried to lead a guy who's stoned and a girl who's completely tripping across a huge field of partying strangers in the half dark, to a pair of blankets that look just like a hundred thousand other pairs of blankets, then clearly you're not me. I was having enough trouble just keeping David, Tina, and Debbie together, much less finding Michael and Willow. The task was not simplified by the fact that David and Tina had their arms around each other, and Tina kept attempting to follow things that only she could see. She was babbling about "celestial guides" and "star energy," while David just kept giggling and saying, "Far out, Teeny. I mean Neeta. Neena. Tina."

Debbie whispered to me, "I have no idea what was in

that water she drank, but I wouldn't have thought Tina knew any of these words. By the way, have you noticed your friend is getting stupider?"

I winced. Truthfully, I had.

Somewhere in our endless trek across the wasted audience lands, Tina stepped on somebody's foot, and David must have stepped on part of someone, too. A male voice barked, "Ow!" A female voice said, "Hey, do you mind watching where you're—David, is that you? Thank goodness, your brother has been worried sick!"

One doesn't generally encounter such a literal case of stumbling upon one's destination, but here we were, standing on our very own blanket. In fact, once Michael sat up, cursing and groaning, I saw that David was standing on his very own brother. Michael had been busy demonstrating how worried sick he was by rolling around, at least half naked, in a sleeping bag with Willow.

Dang, I wanted to be worried sick.

I guess the sixties really were the era of free love, because nobody else seemed to feel the ensuing introductions were at all tinged with awkwardness. Of course, none of them were cursed with the knowledge that they were sitting amid a bizarre cross between a family reunion picnic and a drug-fueled orgy. So that probably helped keep them at ease.

Anyway, orange juice was produced. Another joint was

passed around. A guy named Bert Sommer came onstage and played mellow singer-songwriter music with his band. I said, "No offense, but this doesn't sound very rock-and-roll. He sounds like a Broadway singer."

Debbie said, "Okay, I should have asked what century you were from. He is from Broadway. This is Bert Sommer—from *Hair*! You know, the musical? I saw it, and he was amazing. He's going to be a huge star!"

I was like, *Oh, yeah, he's going to be huge. Mega huge. In the future, we will worship him with monuments and great days of feasting. Wherever cheesy Broadway singers are remembered, his name will be whispered in hushed, reverent tones.* But if I ever write a book called Richie's Dating Bro-tips, Volume I, the very first entry will read:

Never, ever mock a girl's taste in music.

Not that this was a date or anything. I had a girlfriend. Or I would. Several decades hence. Once her parents became sperms and eggs, and then, eventually, people who met and reproduced. So all I said was, "You know who's really going to be huge? Santana. Wait til you see them!"

She said, "I've never even heard of them. How good can they be?"

I just smiled. I knew she would find out in a day or so.

Carlos Santana and his band had been total unknowns at Woodstock—they hadn't even released an album yet—but their performance on Saturday night would basically turn them into superstars.

It was kind of cool knowing that, almost like having a superpower.

Near the end of his set, the Bert guy started playing a Simon and Garfunkel song I recognized called "America," about a young couple that run away together by bus across the country because they feel lost and purposeless. The crowd loved it and gave him a pretty massive standing ovation. Which was awkward for me, because I suddenly noticed that Debbie and I were the only members of the blanket party who weren't too intertwined to stand up.

"Uh, is that okay?" I asked, gesturing vaguely toward the writhing mass of my dad and her friend. (Yes, the sight was exactly as emotionally scarring as it sounds.) "I mean, it's not like Tina is in any shape to, um, give consent or whatever."

It was getting fairly dark, but I could make out Debbie's eyes well enough to know that they were getting kind of misty-looking. "You really are incredibly sweet, Gabriel. You're . . . I don't know . . . chivalrous. I know I teased you before, but it is almost like you're from another time. Like you stepped out of the 1940s, or something."

Wrong direction, I thought.

"Anyway, she's fine. They're just making out. I'll stop it if it gets too out of hand. Your friend doesn't have any diseases, does he?"

Well, at least I could be sure neither of them would catch AIDS, because it hadn't been invented yet. Or discovered. I always get those two mixed up. But I remembered from school that AIDS became a thing in the 1980s. No wonder everybody was so casual about sex in 1969.

"No, he should be okay." I couldn't believe I was serving as my own father's wingman. If I did get back to my own time, I figured I was going to need months of therapy just to get over this one conversation.

We sat back down, and Debbie asked, "So, do you ever feel lost like this? Like there's no hope left in America?"

Wow. I thought of all the historic stuff she had experienced in her childhood: John F. Kennedy, his brother Robert, and Dr. Martin Luther King Jr., all getting assassinated; the constant threat of nuclear war with Russia; civil rights marches, battles, and riots all over the country; the Vietnam conflict; the election of Richard Nixon to the presidency.

I realized, too, that my dad had taught me a ton about his subject without my realizing it.

Anyway, then I thought of all the bad stuff that was still to come: Watergate. President Nixon resigning in disgrace. The end of the Vietnam conflict, with the United States pulling out in defeat. The hippie generation growing up and becoming adults who were just as conservative as every other generation of old people. AIDS. Global warming. 9/11. Afghanistan. Iraq.

Barney.

Miley Cyrus.

"Yeah," I said. "But I don't think it's true. Whenever my father gets upset about stuff in the newspaper or whatever, my mom squeezes his hand and says, 'You're not helping your blood pressure, honey.' Then she says, 'This, too, shall pass.' And I think it always does. I don't know if you can hope for things to get a hundred percent better for the whole planet or anything, but I can guarantee the world isn't going to end anytime soon."

I felt kind of guilty talking about my mom while my dad was snogging with Tina five feet away. Ick.

Debbie hugged her knees and said, "It must be nice to feel so sure."

Glancing over past Dad and Tina, I saw that Michael and Willow were putting up a tiny tent. I assumed they were about to go inside, which would be kind of nice. I didn't want to look at my uncle right then, because unless Jimi and I were going to pull off a miracle together, I knew exactly when Uncle Mike's world was going to end.

"There are a lot of things I don't feel sure about," I said. "Just because I don't think the Russians are about to blow us up doesn't mean I don't worry about stuff."

We talked all through the next act, a guy named Tim

Hardin who was flat-out awful. At some point, Michael and Willow popped back out of the tent, and David and Tina sat back up, so that all six of us were conversing. Willow said, "Wow, that guy is really strung out. It's pretty bad when you can tell from three football fields away in the dark."

I knew just from the train-wreck badness of the sounds emanating from the stage that "strung out" had to be something negative, but I didn't want to ask exactly what it meant, because then Debbie would point out again how I didn't know any of the, ahem, current slang. Fortunately, I'm pretty good with context clues. "Well, it's not like he'd be the first musician ruined by H, right?" David asked.

"H" must be heroin, I figured. It was incredible what experts everyone was on drugs in 1969. And why not? The whole Woodstock was like a giant amateur pharmaceutical research lab.

"Oh, I don't know," Michael said. "Maybe heroin gets a bad rap. You know, the government wants us to believe that all these things are bad for us because they can't control them. They can't tax them, right? Meanwhile, who's making all the money on cigarettes and alcohol, huh? That's right, Uncle Sam. It's just like Vietnam. Follow the money, Davey."

"So what are you saying? We should just get high on everything, all the time, because the government says not to?"

"Well, I'll tell you this, little bro, I haven't seen any of it mess anybody up as bad as alcohol does. Have you?"

These kids were pretty tense, considering. Willow had her hand on the back of Michael's neck, and there was a little brother-to-brother staredown going on. I didn't understand why Michael kept going from happy-go-lucky to bitter and old sounding, but I had seen it a few times over the course of the afternoon and evening. It hit me: When he does this, he sounds like Dad. Future Dad. But that was backward, of course. Future Dad sounded like him. This was the sound of the guy who had trained my father to be bitter.

But why?

Tim Hardin finished up, and Ravi Shankar took the stage. This was something I wanted to see. Ravi Shankar was an Indian classical musician who played a stringed instrument called the sitar. He was the guy who had taught George Harrison all about India's musical instruments and traditions. Without him, the Beatles wouldn't have written some of the most amazing songs ever, and the music of the entire second half of the sixties would have been almost unrecognizably different.

Ravi and two men playing Indian drums got up there and played some amazing trance music. It was completely different from anything I had ever seen. It was around ten at night, and drizzling, but none of us tried to cover up with the blankets or go into the tent or anything. Without really thinking about it, Debbie and I started holding hands, but it wasn't like a sexy thing. It felt more like we had somehow gotten to be old friends already.

Everything felt so peaceful, at least to me.

Michael and Willow had their heads leaning together and their eyes closed, and she was whispering in his ear on and off. I wished I could hear what was going on, because obviously there was something huge I didn't know. But on the other hand, I was really sleepy, and Debbie's hand was really warm, and the music was really nice in a mystical kind of way.

Speaking of mystical, after a while, Tina started feeling another wave of her mystery dosage again, because she began saying stuff like, "Guru, call down the rain! Wet us! Wash us!"

David was saying, "It's okay, Tina, we're all right, we're getting just a little wet and washed. That's good, isn't it?" At the moment, everything was all right with David.

"No, he is calling! The rains will come! Come, O rain! Come and wet us! Come and wash us! Wet us and wash us!"

This was when David committed a drug-fueled tactical error. He imitated Elmer Fudd, the annoying old guy from Bugs Bunny. He shouted, "Wet us and wash us, wascally wabbit!" Then he collapsed backward onto the blanket, cracking up.

Tina was enraged. "He will call down the rain!" she intoned. "The rains will smite you! The rains will wash your soul clean!"

Oh, geez, I thought. *Here we go again with the souls. Nice job, Dad.* Debbie looked pretty exasperated, too. "I should have known this would happen," she said. "You really can't mix stoners with trippers. Am I right?" Willow and Michael both nodded solemnly. Apparently, this was accepted 1960s wisdom, even though it had been lost in the sands of time before I got to age fifteen.

"Tina," Debbie said, "it's cool. The rains are coming, all right? We'll all just watch the music. Everything's groovy, so—"

Then things got freaky. A flash of lightning illuminated the entire field. There was David, still on his back, still grinning. Michael and Willow, together, peering up at the sky in awe. Debbie, her mouth opened in mid-syllable.

And Tina, shrieking. "Here it is! Ten! Nine! Eight!"

She only got down to three before the skies opened up and a pelting storm engulfed us. It didn't last super-long, but by the time it ended, we were six mud-encrusted citizens of a swamped city.

In the eerie, dark silence that followed, Tina turned to David and said, "Told you." Then she threw up on his lap, lay down in the mud, and fell asleep.

I LIVE ONE DAY AT A TIME

FRIDAY, AUGUST 15, 1969

Y ou know the thing at a concert when everybody holds up their cell phone screen or their lighter, or whatever, and waves it back and forth? Did you ever wonder how that happened for the first time? Well, I'm the kind of kid who does wonder about stuff like that, and it used to puzzle me.

Not anymore.

After Tina's eruption, David and I walked over to a row of water pumps we had passed on our way back from the concession stands. I got him washed off as best I could. I felt kind of guilty, because apparently I was wearing his only spare shirt, but to his eternal credit, he didn't ask me to switch or anything. I was quite grateful. I was also thrilled that we found our way back, because it had gotten so dark that our only source of light for navigation was the glow of the mixing desk near our blankets.

When we got back, David fell asleep right beside Tina, soaked shirt and all, and I sat down next to Debbie to watch the next act, a solo singer named Melanie. The stage announcer had noticed the amazing darkness, too, because he said something to the crowd about lighting candles to keep the rain away. It was incredible: At some point during one of Melanie's songs, I looked around and the entire bowl we were sitting in was alight with flickering, wavering candle flames.

"Wow, that's new," Debbie said.

"What do you mean?" I asked. "Don't people do this at concerts all the time?"

"Do what?"

"You know. Light stuff and wave it around?"

"No, of course not. Otherwise, why would I have said, 'That's new'?"

"Uh, right. I, um, well, my parents don't let me go to concerts much."

My mind was boggling. This was so cool! Yet again, I was the only person in the whole place who knew what we were witnessing. If I ever got back to my own time, and if my parents ever ungrounded me, and if they ever actually allowed me to go to a concert, I knew I would never be able to see cell phones being hoisted aloft during an encore without smiling a secret smile.

I knew the next singer, but only because of his last name. He was Arlo Guthrie. His father, Woody Guthrie, was the folk singer who had written "This Land Is Your Land." Woody had died tragically of a terrible genetic disease called Huntington's disease, which makes its victims go insane at some point in their adult lives without any warning after totally normal childhoods. I remembered hearing about Arlo's case, because he had had to grow up not knowing whether he would inherit his father's condition. In the end, he had been fine, but I was pretty sure he hadn't known that yet at the time of Woodstock.

What would it be like to know there was a fifty-fifty chance you'd suddenly go insane, with no chance of a cure?

As Arlo was getting ready to play, Debbie said, "I'd hate to be him."

It felt kind of great to finally know what she was talking about. "The disease?"

"Yeah. I mean, how do you live, knowing it might all be for nothing?"

"Why would it be for nothing?" I asked. "I mean, he's getting to play at the biggest concert in history. He's a famous singer. He sounds like he's having fun up there, right? Isn't that something? Whatever happens later, doesn't this matter?" Actually, Arlo sounded like he was completely high. Between songs, his voice was all sniffly and giggly, his words were strangely elongated, and he kept losing his train of thought.

"Well, but . . . okay, what if you knew right now that you had even odds of getting Huntington's disease? Would you bother to study in school? Would you bust your butt in college, or would you drop out and go live on a commune somewhere? I think I might just drop out and stay high, or something."

I thought about that. It was hard to ignore what I knew: that Arlo Guthrie was not going to go insane. As far as I remembered, he would still be plugging away, old and white-haired, singing these same old songs on Woodstock reunion tours in the 2010s. "But then, what if you did screw around and mess up your future, and you never got sick?"

We sat for a while, listening to the music and wondering together what it would be like to be semi-doomed. Then I looked over at my sleeping father, and my uncle's legs sticking out of his tent, and asked Debbie, "What if you could know?"

"Could know what?"

"Your fate. Would you want to?"

"What do you mean?"

"Well, let's say you were Woody Guthrie, and there was some kind of blood test you could take that would let you know for sure whether you were going to get the disease or not later on. Would you want to know, or would you want to wait and see?"

"Shit, Gabriel, that's hard. I couldn't do anything to change the results, right?"

I shook my head.

"And I wouldn't be able to forget them once I knew them. AND there's no treatment for the disease, so knowing in advance doesn't do any good, right?"

I shook my head again.

"Yup, I'd just stay high." She laughed, but it wasn't a ha-ha kind of laugh. I wondered about David and Michael. Was my uncle doomed, or semi-doomed like Arlo Guthrie? Could I change Michael's fate, or was it already written somewhere? And if I couldn't change it, would he want to know what was coming? Was there any point in trying to influence anything that happened this weekend? Was I here to tell my uncle something, to tell my father something, or to learn something for myself?

Another thing hit me: What if Michael knew exactly what was going to happen? What if he already was planning to kill himself, and this was his big last party weekend? Maybe going to Woodstock with his girlfriend and his brother was Michael's version of staying high. If so, I just didn't get it. He was definitely on edge at times about something—I had seen that. But he had calmed down again as soon as Willow had touched him. And yeah, he had awful parents, but so did my father. And clearly, my dad was going to make it to adulthood. Plus, Michael had Willow.

Just then, Willow's leg wrapped around Michael's, and even over the music, I could have sworn I heard a little groaning noise coming from the tent. I felt a blush spread across my face. I absolutely didn't get it.

The last performer of the night was a folk singer, Joan Baez. I didn't know too much about her, other than that she had an old-fashioned kind of voice that had always annoyed me on my parents' old records. I turned to Debbie and said, "She's not very rock-and-roll, either, is she? Kinda like that Broadway dude."

Debbie almost bit my head off. "Gabriel, show some respect. She's Joan Baez. She's my idol. She played with Dr. Martin Luther King at the March on Washington. She was fighting for civil rights when we were still learning to spell."

I was stunned. "Uh . . ." I replied intelligently. In my defense, I hadn't even been alive when Debbie had been learning to spell, so what did she expect?

"And do you know where her husband, David, is now? Right now, while she's standing up there onstage, pregnant, her husband is in prison for refusing to register for the draft. She's a real American hero. So don't mock her, all right?"

"I'm sorry," I said. "I didn't know."

After a few really political songs, with speeches in between, I built up the courage to speak again. "So, uh, do you know anybody who's been drafted?"

"My cousin Marty. Last we heard, he was with the Hundred and First Airborne, getting dropped by helicopter right in the middle of jungle firefights."

Wow, I had never known a single person who was in the army. Even though I had lived through the wars in Iraq and Afghanistan, they hadn't really touched my life. I didn't know what to say.

"And my other cousin, Frankie. He came home last year pretty messed up. He has three Purple Hearts. From what my aunt told my mom, he got shot in one leg trying to save his buddy, but then the guy died anyway. Then when Frankie recovered, he got sent back to his unit, and the boy in front of him stepped on a mine. A piece of the kid's helmet sliced into Frankie's arm and cut an artery. He needed something like sixty stitches, but the army sent him back out to fight again. The third Purple Heart, nobody will even tell me about. I heard my parents whispering once, and I almost got the feeling he might've shot himself to avoid going back out into the jungle again. All I know is, since he got back, he doesn't do anything but sit in his old room and listen to the Doors. It's really sad."

I wondered what the draft meant for my father, and for millions of kids just like him all across the country. It occurred to me that, in a way, my dad was an Arlo Guthrie, but Vietnam was his disease: He was going through high school, studying or not studying, trying or not trying, without knowing whether he would just get drafted and sent to Vietnam at the end anyway. How many of the guys around me were worried about the draft at that very moment? How many had already fought in the war and come back? How many would flee to Canada, or go to jail, rather than report for duty? How many would die?

Of course, I wondered again whether it would be better or worse for a man to know his fate. With a whisper, I could release my dad from worrying about getting drafted, but if I could get him to believe I could really see the future, then I'd have to tell him about his brother. It was a pretty classic no-win situation.

Joan Baez sang a duet with some guy then, and they made a big deal out of dedicating it to someone. I was too lost in thought to catch the dedication, though. "Wow," Debbie said, "it's pretty funny that they're singing a song for that idiot Ronald Reagan."

"You mean President Reagan?" I asked.

"Don't even joke around like that," she said. "It's bad enough he's the governor of California. I can't even stand to imagine he could ever get elected president."

A few songs later, Joan handed her guitar off to somebody, stood alone in a spotlight, and sang a totally a capella version of "Swing Low, Sweet Chariot" that felt like a magic spell. I could feel a silent awakening all around me. David woke up and sat upright; Michael and Willow stuck their heads out of the tent. I know I said her voice had always bugged me, but suddenly, hearing it here, I understood. I don't know how to explain it, except to tell you this: When Joan Baez sang about a sweet chariot coming to carry her home, half a million people felt like we were riding right along with her.

Michael put one arm around David and one around Willow. As soon as the song ended, he said, "I'm glad we're here together. Remember this, okay? Just promise me you'll remember this."

Joan put her guitar back on and started singing "We Shall Overcome," the last song of the first night of Woodstock. Debbie lit a match and squinted at her watch. "Hey," she whispered, "it's almost two in the morning!"

At the edges of the dim matchstick glow, I could just make out the smiles on the faces all around our little circle. Out of nowhere, I suddenly felt a tear running down my own cheek as the match blew out. Without a word being said, Debbie curled into my shoulder to sleep, and I lay there thinking about Michael . . . and the sixty-two days he had left.

MORNING SUNRISE

SATURDAY, AUGUST 16, 1969

It rained on and off during the night, so by the time I woke up, our blankets had begun to sink and slide in the mud. The right side of me was tangled up with Debbie, and would have felt somewhat warm and snuggly if her head hadn't cut off all the circulation in that arm. Also, that hip was throbbing where the hood ornament had nailed me the day before, and her knee was somehow curled up against that exact spot. Meanwhile, my left side was hanging off the blanket, and that hand and foot were sucked into little mini-vortexes of gritty, slick mud.

It wasn't one of my comfier wake-ups, although Debbie would have felt kind of sweet against me if I hadn't been numb, tingly, and throbbing all at once.

Oh, and I had to pee like a madman.

Escape was a necessity. I lay there for a moment, attempting to gather my wits. I got a whiff of the air around me, and noted two things. First, half a million smoking, drinking, partying people getting rained on all night in a titanically huge cow pasture, between long rows of portable toilets, creates a fairly stupendous odor—picture what it would smell like if the Goodyear Blimp dropped thousands of tons of manure inches in front of your face just as you climbed out the bathroom window of the world's most revolting greasy fast-food restaurant. Behind a garbage dump. Next door to a smokers' convention. Second, Tina's orange juice-scented puke cut right through the general funk with a power all its own.

It wasn't even dawn yet, but I could see by the faint, diffuse light around me that nobody around me was awake. I got my arm and leg free from Debbie's—which was like playing Twister with two completely immovable limbs—as gently as I could. She snorted, but didn't open her eyes. Debbie was kind of a sweet snorter.

David was on the other side of Debbie, sandwiched between her and a face-planted Tina. Not only did I have to escape, but I had to drag him with me. Whatever attempts he had made to rinse his shirt the night before had been rendered completely ineffective by his sleeping arrangements. Even in the dim half-light, I could see that he and his date were both centered in a dried pool of recycled citrus.

I remembered from the Woodstock movie that there was a big pond somewhere downhill behind the stage, where people had gone skinny-dipping throughout the weekend. I figured David and I could grab some soap, and maybe some tooth-brushing supplies. Then, if we hurried, we could get down to the water and clean ourselves off before most other people were even awake.

Because there was one thing I was sure of: I had to make sure my dad's clothes got super-duper clean before he started looking around for his spare outfit and realized it was on me. I'm not even a big fan of orange juice when it's new.

I tapped David on the shoulder and whispered in his ear to explain the plan. He nodded after a moment and stumbled to his feet. His pants and shirt made a sickly *swick!* noise as they peeled away from the blanket. Then he grabbed his backpack, and we started walking down toward the stage. If I remembered correctly, we would have to walk around behind the stage and pass into a little wooded area to reach the water.

Progress was slow, and we definitely caused a few sleepy people to cry, "Hey, watch it, mannnnn!" However, we made it onto the road that edged around the stage, passed under the huge wooden walkway that the musicians traveled to get onstage, and found our way down to the water. Sure enough, we were the only people there.

It was a little bit lighter at this point, so that I could get a decent look at David. He needed more than a little splashing-off action. Aside from his involuntary vitamin C rinse, he was also so covered with mud from head to toe that he resembled an extra from a zombie movie. Glancing down at my own clothing, I realized that being pinned down by Debbie all night had kept me partially clean; only my left side had the zombie makeover look. Still, we were a hot mess.

I started taking off my shirt. What had to happen next was horrifying, but unavoidable. We were going to have to take it all off and do some major scrubbing if we were going to survive this weekend—and we were going to have to do it fast, before the world's biggest nude swim party started up again for the day.

"David," I said, "do you have any soap, or shampoo, or something?"

"Yeah, sure," he said. "Michael's an Eagle Scout. He packed a whole survival kit. We've got soap, shampoo, baking soda for emergency toothpaste. . . ."

"Okay, perfect, let's strip and scrub."

He looked at me kind of funny, almost like I had woken him up at six a.m. after a wild party night, dragged him to a secluded pond, and ordered him to strip. "What?"

"We have to strip and get clean."

"Strip?"

I sighed. I reminded myself that he didn't know we were

going to be in the middle of one of the world's most in-famous nude movie scenes if we didn't hurry. "Yes. Listen: I'm wearing your only spare clothes, right?"

He nodded.

"Well, look at them."

He did.

"And it was incredibly nice of you to lend them to me, but . . . uh . . . they're pretty messed up now, and even if you did want them back like this, I don't have anything to change into. So I have to get them clean, right?"

He nodded again. I noticed I could see the white of his teeth now. The sun was going to break out over the trees any minute.

"And take a look at your clothing. Do you remember what Tina did to your shirt last night?"

He looked down and his face squinched up. He remembered.

"So, all I'm saying is we have to take off all these clothes and scrub them with whatever you've got, and we've got to do it fast, before a ton of other people come wandering down here with the same idea. What do you say?"

David didn't answer. He just shucked off his sneakers, and grabbed the bar of soap in one hand. I took off my sneakers, pants, and underwear, bundled all of my clothes under one arm, and picked up the shampoo bottle. Then I walked into the shallows of the pond. David followed.

Skinny-dipping is pretty darn awkward, especially with just one other guy, because honestly, there is no good place to look. We both stared very intently at our clothes as we scrubbed at top speed, which worked pretty well except when we had to pass the soap. At those moments, we just sort of laughed sheepishly.

Still, it felt amazing to get clean.

Just as the sun started hitting the tips of the trees, I got a good look at my bruised hip. It was pretty crazy: I had a perfect imprint of the Cadillac ornament branded into my skin. It occurred to me that I might have that mark forever.

Swell. There's nothing like a big old tattoo of an old-people car symbol to drive the babes wild.

When David and I had gotten both ourselves and our clothes clean, I forgot about the bruise for one glorious moment of pure, radiant joy. My plan had worked. We had gotten cleaned up, and had the whole pond to ourselves. The warm sun struck me full in the face as I strode forth from the water. I dropped my clothing in the reeds onshore and stood with my eyes closed for a while, enjoying the feeling of being all alone with the brand-new day. I even spread my arms to enjoy the rays.

That was when a female voice shouted, from about three feet in front of me, "Far out! Skinny-diiiiippppp!!!!!!!"

I opened my eyes, and saw first tens, then hundreds of

teenagers swarming past me, ripping off their clothes as they went. At first, I wanted to die of embarrassment, but then I burst out laughing as a realization swept over me.

Yes, thank you, ladies and gentlemen. Now you know my place in history. I, Richard Gabriel Barber, started the skinny-dipping at Woodstock.

David and I walked back up the hill past the stage and found that Willow and Michael hadn't emerged from the tent yet. Tina was sitting up, hugging her knees and staring off into space. Debbie was standing next to her, scanning the horizon in all directions. She laughed when she saw us.

"Hey," she said, "we just got back from brushing our teeth at the pumps. What happened to you? You're soaked!" she said.

"We went for a little morning clean-up swim," I said. "I didn't want to wake you."

"You swam in your clothes?" she asked, grinning mischievously.

"Nope," I said, grinning back.

"In that case," she said, "you definitely should have woken me up. We could have had fun."

Ahhh, I thought, *I love the sixties.* "Are you hungry?" I asked her.

"Starved. Why?"

David said, "Well, some girls by the water told us about

a place over the hill that's serving breakfast to anyone who wants some."

"Wait," Debbie said, "there were other girls swimming naked down there?"

"Ummm . . ." I said. "Not exactly. We got out, and then they got in."

"So they just saw you naked."

I nodded.

"And then you saw them naked."

I stayed very, very still.

"And you talked to them?"

"He didn't," David said. "I did."

Hey, I thought. *That's the first time my father has ever stuck up for me.* It felt good.

Debbie, David, and I stood and stared at each other awkwardly for a moment, until Tina piped up. "Hey," she asked my dad, "aren't you that guy that kept laughing last night?"

He nodded.

She reached over and smacked him on the leg. "Well, thanks for keeping me grounded. You really helped. Now, did someone say something about breakfast? For some reason, I have the weirdest craving for orange juice!"

TWO WORLDS

SATURDAY, AUGUST 16, 1969

The forest was amazing, like a whole alternate universe. There were trails everywhere, with signs like *Groovy Way* and *High Way*. People had set up booths, some of which were selling arts and crafts, and some of which were selling a mind-blowing variety of drugs right out in the open. I was so used to life in the 2010s that I kept waiting for a zillion federal agents to come rappelling down out of the trees, Taser everyone in sight, and throw us all into the back of a bunch of black vans. Of course, I had also been arrested the day before, which might have added to my paranoia, but still . . . times had definitely changed.

We asked a bunch of people we passed where we could find the food kitchen, and they directed us out into a clearing where long lines of sleepy-looking people were waiting. The lines moved pretty well, though, and soon we each had our very own paper cups of granola and juice. We sat down under some trees and munched away as we watched the strange woodland goings-on. Just in our little field of vision, a nude guy was leading a hundred or so people in a morning yoga class; some other dude was chasing a real live goat around and around a tree; and a bunch of dirty, naked toddlers were laughing and running through a playground.

"Check out those kids," Tina said. "Imagine if your parents were cool enough to take you to something like this."

"Yeah," Debbie said, "then we could have told them the truth about where we are this weekend!"

"Oh, man," David said. "My parents know where I am. They just don't care . . . as long as I'm not in the house bugging them! For them, this is a party weekend."

We all just sat there for a while, munching loudly, until Tina looked at me and asked, "What about you, Gabriel?"

"Uh, it's kind of hard to explain, but . . . well, one of my parents knows where I am. Kind of. I mean, not entirely. Exactly. I— I guess I'm trying to say, my parents wouldn't exactly approve if they totally knew."

"Thanks for clearing that up, Gabriel," Debbie said. "Funny, I thought you were the honest type."

"I am," I said. *Usually,* I thought. "It's just . . . I really had to be here. Seriously, I felt like I had no choice. It was my destiny. I can deal with the consequences later. Haven't you ever just had to do something?"

"Yeah, this!" Debbie said. She crumpled her granola cup, threw it aside, and kissed me full on the mouth. David and Tina applauded. *Wow*, I thought. *This isn't the kind of thing that randomly happens to me. Blondes really do have more fun!* I couldn't decide whether to get really into it and ask for seconds, die of embarrassment, or propose a nice late-morning swim.

Ultimately, I went with the swim. Debbie had been right. Skinny-dipping was a lot more interesting with her along.

The whole middle of the day alternated between rain and shine, but we all had a great time anyway. Eventually, Michael and Willow woke up, just in time to serve us a late lunch and watch the afternoon's bands.

At some point Willow, Tina, and Debbie all went off to wait in line for the bathrooms, which left me with my dad and uncle to watch a guy named Country Joe McDonald. Country Joe got the crowd's attention with a rowdy cheer that started with "Gimme an 'F' . . . . Gimme a 'U' . . ." and then burst into the strongest anti-Vietnam song of the whole weekend. It was called the "I-Feel-Like-I'm-Fixin'-to-Die Rag" and featured the line "Be the first one on your block to have your boy come home in a box."

People went crazy for him. It made me feel kind of sad

for my generation, because it seems to me that we don't really have a cause or spokespeople in the same way my dad's did. Then again, I wondered whether I was making too much of one song, because at that moment, Michael went into the tent, fished around in his bags, and came out with another lit joint. "Too much heavy politics, man," he said. "We're here to give my brother a good time. Right, Davey?"

I kept refusing the pot when it got to me, but it didn't take David and Michael long to polish it off. This time David didn't get all giggly. Instead, he got mellow and started reminiscing with Michael about their childhood. "Hey, Mikey," he said, "do you remember that time in kindergarten when you caught that frog for me? And I asked you if it would live forever?"

Michael smiled. "And I promised you it would."

"Yeah. And then it died. So you caught me another one and didn't tell me."

"Yup."

"And that kept happening for, like, a year?"

"Yup."

"You know what, Mikey? I never told you this, but really, even then, I kind of knew. 'Cause the spots on those frogs were in all different places. And Mrs. Gross read my class a story about how leopards never change their spots, right? So one day I went up to her desk at recess time and I asked her whether frogs ever change their spots, and she said no, not as far as she knew. And then I thought, 'Wow, I discovered a new species of frog!' "

Mike laughed and rubbed his brother's hair. "You were always such a funny kid, Davey," he said. "Stay funny, okay?"

I felt my eyes stinging.

The girls were gone for more than two hours, which meant they missed the entire next act, another solo guitar player named John Sebastian, whose music I really liked. Then a heavy blues-rock group called the Keef Hartley Band came on, and I saw another new side of my father: the drummer geek.

"Check this out, Gabriel," he said. "Keef Hartley is supposed to be a really good drummer. He replaced Ringo Starr in Rory Storm and the Hurricanes when Ringo quit to join the Beatles! And then he played in John Mayall and the Bluesbreakers!"

I was like, *Hey, that's obscure. Dad talks about drummers like I talk about guitarists.*

Meanwhile, Michael and I bonded over the guitar sounds. "Hey, do you hear that lead tone?" he asked. "That's beautiful, man. It's gotta be a Telecaster neck pickup!"

Of course, we were too far away to see what guitar anybody was playing, which almost made me wish for the gigantic Jumbotrons of the 2010s. I was pretty good at telling apart the sounds of different guitars, but I wasn't sure.

"How can you tell? I play guitar, too, and I can hear that it's a single coil, but why not a Strat?"

"With a Strat, you can hear the whammy bar springs in the sound. Trust me, it's a Tele. Wanna get closer and see?"

"Uh, sure."

"David, do you want to come?"

"Nah," David said. "I want to wait here for the girls." Truthfully, David looked too blissed-out to move.

"All right," Michael told him, "you can watch our stuff. Just don't go anywhere, okay?"

It got more and more crowded as we got closer to the stage, and I started to feel a bit too much like a sardine, but Michael was really determined to check out the lead guitarist's gear. With a lot of *excuse me*s, we eventually got close enough that if I really squinted, I could see that he had been right about the guitar, which was, indeed, a Fender Telecaster. I was impressed.

"Wow, you have golden ears," I said. Actually, I half-shouted it, because the music was way louder this close to the stage. But this was my first chance to talk with my legendary uncle alone, so I didn't mind expending a little extra effort. "Hey, your brother told me you're in a band together."

"Were," he said. "The other guys don't know it yet, but I'm gone."

"Gone? What happened? Are you going away to college?"

He snorted. "Me? College? I don't think so!"

I didn't know what to say. My dad was so big on education, I had just kind of assumed college would have been part of my uncle's plans if things hadn't gone off the rails somehow.

Michael ran a hand through his hair. "Listen, I don't even really know you, all right?" he said. "But Willow gets . . . feelings about people sometimes. She told me she thinks we met you for a reason. Crazy, right?"

What was I supposed to say to that? "Um, I don't think Willow's crazy. I think she's amazing." *What the heck,* I figured. *Half-truths have been working great for me so far.*

"And you know something else? I didn't tell my brother or Willow this, but I wasn't looking down at the radio when we hit you. I was looking right at the road. I didn't just say you appeared in front of the car—I meant that you literally appeared in front of the car. I'm talking, like, BOOM! Flash of light—instant kid!"

I didn't say anything.

He ran that hand through his hair again. He looked like he was about to jump out of his own skin. "I don't know, maybe Willow's not the crazy one. Maybe I'm finally going insane. Between all the shit from my old man, and the letter, and what's going to happen to Davey when I'm—"

What letter? In all the piles of my uncle's stuff, I hadn't seen a letter, and nobody had mentioned anything about any drama with a letter before this.

"Wow, man, you must think I'm crazy. First, I run you over with a damn Caddy, then I tell you I didn't see you until you suddenly appeared in front of the car like some kind of crazy Captain Kirk. And now I'm laying this whole trip on you about my life, and you probably have no idea what I'm even talking about!"

I still just stood there. It felt like anything I said would be the wrong thing.

"Come on, kid. Say something!"

I flashed the dorky *Star Trek* hand signal. "Um, I come in peace?"

He smiled, but didn't laugh. "I'm serious."

"Okay, you're right. I don't think it's just random chance that I met you and your brother. I think I was meant to be here for a reason. I swear I don't want to do anything bad to either of you. All I want is to help. Can you trust me?"

As the Keef Hartley Band wailed away a hundred feet from us, my uncle Mike stared into my eyes for a disturbingly long time. Then he took hold of both my shoulders and said, "I do trust you. I do. But if you hurt my brother, I swear I will haunt you forever."

He was *going* to haunt me? He couldn't know how he had already haunted my entire life. Every hair on my body stood on end. "Michael," I said, "you mentioned a letter. Can you tell me about it?"

TEEN ANGEL

SATURDAY, AUGUST 16, 1969

"I can't tell you about the letter," Michael said. His face looked absolutely ravaged. Whatever had been tormenting my father since 1969, this letter had to be part of it. I needed to know.

"Why not?"

"Because . . . because . . . listen, my brother can't even know about this. I'm sorry. I know I said I trust you, but I meant I trust you to hang with us for the weekend, share our food, watch David's back when he's high. But if you slip and tell him about the letter, he wouldn't be safe around our father if . . ."

Half a song went by.

"If?"

"If anything happened to me."

Oh, shit. This was it. "Michael, listen to me," I said. "You have to tell me about the letter. I swear you can trust me. Willow was right. I don't know exactly how it happened, but I did just appear out of thin air in front of your car to help you."

"Prove it."

"All right." *Great,* I thought. *How am I supposed to prove that?* Then I realized I probably could at least make Michael believe I could see the future. I grabbed his sleeve and dragged him through the crowd to the nearest guy in a Woodstock uniform. "Hey, who's playing next?" I asked.

"Some band called Santana!" the guy shouted back.

Perfect. Because I had spent about a million hours practicing guitar along with *Santana: The Woodstock Experience* on my iPod. "Michael, if I predict every single song in order, and sing along with the drum solo, which by the way will be in the seventh song, then will you believe I might, umm, have been sent here?"

"Uhh, sure, I guess so. Or I might just believe somebody laced my weed with something, man."

I laughed. "No, I am dead serious. Listen, I will make you a deal: If I convince you I know what's coming during this next band's set, then you have to tell me about the letter. But there's one other thing. You have to promise me you won't tell your brother anything about this, okay? He can't know. That's really, really important. I don't know exactly what would happen if he found out, but I know it would be a huge disaster. Deal?"

"Deal," he said.

For the second-to-last time, I shook hands with my uncle Mike.

We started back toward the blankets, and I asked, "What did you mean about your brother not being safe around your father?" I had tried a million times to imagine the kinds of neglect my dad must have suffered as a kid, but it had never occurred to me that he might have been abused, too.

"Listen," Michael said, "our dad smacks me around all the time, okay? But he only ever hit David once that I can remember. It was on a Sunday morning when we were pretty little. Mom and Dad were sleeping late, and Davey was hungry. I looked through the cabinets for something to give him, but there wasn't really anything. So I decided to run down to the store.

"You have to understand, this kind of thing happened all the time. I would go into my dad's wallet or my mom's purse and take a dollar or two. Usually, they carried a bunch of cash around, and they never remembered exactly how much they had spent on a night when they had gone out, so it wasn't like they were going to catch me stealing from them.

"This one time, though, Dad only had a twenty in his wallet. Mom woke up while I was gone, and asked David where I was. He said he didn't know. Then she woke Dad up, and he asked David again where I was. David said again that he didn't know. Dad must have looked in his wallet, because David told me later that he started shouting about how his last twenty was gone.

"When I walked in, I was carrying a loaf of bread, a jug of milk, and a dozen eggs. I had eighteen bucks in my front pocket, and a penny piece of bubblegum in my mouth. Mom, Dad, and Davey were standing in the kitchen, waiting for me.

"First, Dad slapped me across the face, and I dropped the eggs. He called me a 'goddamned sneak-thief.' Next, he smacked David. I kept trying to say, 'Davey was hungry,' but Dad just kept getting madder and madder. Then Mom snatched the bread and milk from me and started in about how now she had to clean up the eggs. So then they were both shouting, and Davey was still just standing there, holding his face with one hand, his little stomach with the other, and looking at the bread like he had never seen food before."

Listening to Michael's story made me ashamed. I thought about times when I had wasted food and my dad had yelled at me about it. Years too late, I understood.

"So I tried to give him a piece of the bread, but Dad flipped out even more. He said, 'Oh, Davey was so hungry, you had to go out and spend my last goddamned twenty dollars on gum for yourself, huh?' Then he whirled around, grabbed David's arm, and said, 'You knew! You knew where your lying thief of a brother was! I think one no-good liar is enough for this family, don't you? But if you're going to share his lies, you can share his breakfast, too!

"Then Dad forced my lips open, yanked out my gum, and shoved it into David's mouth. It was horrible. And he wouldn't let David eat anything—or spit out that gum—all day. Even now, Davey can't look at a stick of gum.

"If Dad went that insane over a penny's worth of gum, he's going to want to kill over what's in this letter. And that's why Davey can't know about the letter. Because my father will know about the letter, and when he does find out he's going to want someone to blame. That someone can . . . not . . . be . . . David. I don't care anymore what happens to me, but David doesn't get blamed for anything I do, ever again."

Wow. My father had always made a huge issue of not letting me chew gum, which I had thought was completely psychotic and random. I had gotten explosively furious at him so many times for his weird little rules. Now I knew that for the rest of my life, whenever he came up with some restriction that seemed bizarre, I was going to picture little-kid Dad chewing gum in that kitchen, and try really hard to bite my tongue.

"All right," I said. "Let's not worry about the letter right now." Every time my father or Michael told me anything about their home life, I just wanted to curl up in a corner and cry. I decided that, if Michael's mission was to give David the most awesome Woodstock weekend possible, maybe I could start by just promising to help out with that. It wouldn't make up for the gum torture, but it was something I knew I could deliver.

After all, I was pretty darn sure I could deliver Jimi freaking Hendrix.

"Listen, Michael, you want your brother to have a weekend he'll never, ever forget, right?"

He swallowed, then said, "Yeah. I promised."

"Then here's what I promise you: Within the next twenty-four hours, you and your brother will be on a first-name basis with at least one major rock star."

"Seriously?"

"Seriously." Unless my time travel had messed everything up, in which case, we wouldn't meet Jimi, and I'd be stuck here forever. But then I also wouldn't be born, in which case I wouldn't ever get to come back here in the first place, in which case . . . "I mean, I'm ninety-nine percent sure. Well, ninety-eight. Well, umm, maybe you shouldn't mention anything to David, just in case. But yeah. I think so. Hey, we'd better get back to everybody else before Santana starts. By the way, Santana will be playing a superb-sounding Gibson SG. He'll have a bunch of percussionists, a keyboard guy, and an African American bass player with a rockin' Abe Lincoln beard."

"What the hell are you talking about?"

"An Abe Lincoln beard? It's like a normal beard, but without the mustache part. You know, sort of Amish looking?"

"Yeah, I know what Abe Lincoln's beard looked like. What's an African American?"

Whoa. Slang crisis alert. "Uh, he's black."

"Willow was right about one thing: You talk funny. Where are you from again?"

"Maybe I'll tell you sometime. But I think I'll wait until you're either not high, or a whole lot higher than you are now. I'm not sure which."

When we got back to the blankets, the girls were back, and everybody was guzzling down a bunch of Cokes that they had brought back from their travels. Debbie tossed one to me, and I noticed again how much better 1969 Coke tasted. It had to be the real sugar.

Mom had always said high fructose corn syrup was poisoning every cell in my body, but she had never told me it was also so much less delicious than what it had replaced.

Anyway, a couple of minutes after we sat down, Santana started playing. I named the first couple of songs for Michael and sang the guitar lines in his ear, but then I had to stop, because I had to live in the moment. Yes, I had been listening to these exact performances on my iPod for years, but the difference between that and seeing them live in the middle of a huge audience that was experiencing Santana for the first time was like the difference between being shown a sketch of the most beautiful girl in the world dancing, and actually dancing with her. Because we danced. So did everybody as far as I could see. You couldn't not dance.

Then came the seventh song, "Soul Sacrifice," which may have been the most musically exciting eleven minutes and thirty-five seconds of my entire existence. I couldn't resist; I stopped dancing with Debbie for a moment, tapped David on the shoulder, and said, "Check out the drummer. His name is Michael Shrieve, and he's a teenager. He's going to play a solo in this song that will blow—your—mind!"

David was dancing with Tina. He leaned over and shouted in my ear, "How do you know?"

"I, uh, saw these guys at the Fillmore East in New York a few months ago. This song is the drummer's big solo showcase."

When the solo came, David stopped dead in his tracks. Michael Shrieve started out loud and fast, then got slower and slower, quieter and quieter. Next, he built back up to a roar so powerful and pulsating that it didn't seem possible it could be coming from a single person with only four limbs. Tina wrapped herself around David's neck and kind of nibbled at him, but he was completely absorbed. I knew my father when he had that level of concentration, and I was pretty sure Tina could have stripped down and done a full-frontal tackle without getting him to tear his attention away from the stage.

When the band finally broke back in and played the climax of the song, David turned to me in awe. "That was worth the whole weekend. He's the best drummer I've ever seen!"

I just smiled. I had witnessed my dad concentrating that hard a million times, but I had never, ever witnessed him in awe. He was right; it was worth the whole weekend.

Santana played one more song after that, then left the stage to the most thunderous applause I had heard all weekend. I think the three Barbers clapped the loudest. Then my uncle put his arm around me, pulled me close, and whispered in my ear, "I believe."

HIGH TIME

SATURDAY, AUGUST 16, 1969

R ight after Santana's set, Michael and Willow passed around our dinner: peanut butter, crackers, and bread. We had a few spoons to share, but no clean plates left, so things got pretty messy pretty fast. Of course, we had already spent the day traipsing through ankle-deep mud and getting drizzled on intermittently, so it wasn't like anybody was pristine to begin with.

And the meal tasted delicious.

Next, Willow brought out a tinfoil-wrapped square with a candle lying sideways on top of it. Smiling mischievously, she said, "If you kids are ready for some special dessert, I brought something from home for Davey. His sixteenth birthday is in two weeks, and Mike and I talked about taking him on a birthday trip after we get back home, but I'll probably have a new job by then, so . . . well . . . I decided it would be cool to celebrate now."

Michael said, "But before you open this up, Willow, I need the kids to promise me something. Guys, I need you all to swear you'll stay right here on these blankets and stick together for the rest of the night, all right?"

We all looked around at each other. I didn't know what everybody else was thinking, but I was like, *Uh, what's the big deal? It's a cake, not a suicide mission.*

"Seriously, do you swear you'll hang out right here?"

David said, "I swear."

Tina and Debbie made eye contact with each other, shrugged in unison, and mumbled together, "I swear."

I wasn't going anywhere without my father and uncle anyway, so I swore, too. Willow opened up the foil to reveal a huge, uncut sheet of brownies. Michael stuck the candle in the middle and lit it. Willow said, "Make a wish, Davey!"

My father stood up, closed his eyes, and blew with all his might. Willow and Michael enveloped him in a hug, and I heard Michael's muffled voice say, "Be good this year, Davey. Be safe."

Then Willow elbowed Michael out of the way and kissed David right on the lips. "That's one to grow on," she said. David blushed, and Michael laughed.

As soon as Willow put the brownies down in the middle of the blankets, David started tearing off a big chunk. Michael said, "Not so much, Davey. Go slow." I thought that was strange too, but by then I was getting used to Michael being a bit of a mother hen when it came to David. David broke off some of his massive slab for me, and then distributed pieces for the girls, too. He held out a hunk to his brother, but Michael held up a hand and said, "Save me some. The original plan was for us to eat these with you, but now that you have friends your age here . . . Willow and I are going to go to the forest for a little while, but we'll be back for the Grateful Dead. Remember: Stay here."

They walked off together, and we ate our dessert. I had to say, the brownies tasted a little stale. They almost seemed moldy or something, but I didn't want to ruin David's birthday fest by mentioning it, so I just swallowed mine as fast as I could and tried not to think too hard about the aftertaste. Willow was still the hottest human female on the entire planet, but baking did not appear to be her strong suit.

The strange thing was that Debbie, Tina, and David just munched down those brownies like they didn't notice the funkiness. Maybe Betty Crocker hadn't gotten her technology quite right yet by 1969?

Whatever. I forgot all about the primitive state of 1960s dessert technology when the next band took the stage, because Debbie suddenly started kissing me. You know how different girls have different kissing styles? Well, Debbie's was "Ambush!"

It was kind of fun.

We kissed our way through the Incredible String Band, who truthfully were much less incredible than Debbie's lips. At first, the kissing was making me crazy to go farther. If my dad hadn't been sitting five feet away, I don't know what might have happened. As it was, a heated argument broke out between my inner lust demon and my conscience anyway:

Now put one hand behind her head and lie down. Come on, boy—do it in one smooth motion. You know you want to!

Unnngghhhh! I doooooo. But I can't! What . . . about . . . Courtney?

There is no Courtney . . . yet. In this time, there is only pleasure.

But . . . we'll never see each other again. That's . . . that's . . .

I believe the word you seek is "perfect"!

I tried to concentrate on the music, but I didn't know any of this band's songs, and they were just too mellow to be a strong distraction from Debbie. Who was now licking my left ear. My eyes rolled up into my head, and Debbie guided me backward onto the blanket. When my eyes came back down, I was looking straight up into the pre-sunset sky.

Which appeared to be on fire. Now this was a distraction!

"Debbie!"

"Mmmmm . . . what?" she said throatily.

"Fire!"

"You feel it, too?" she whispered in my ear.

Despite myself, I shivered. Debbie was an awesome whisperer. "No, I mean fire. Like, a firey fire. The kind with flames."

Debbie giggled. "God, I'm better at this than I thought," she murmured.

It took all the willpower I had, but I pulled away from her lips. "Debbie," I said, "look up!"

She lay back next to me and looked straight up. "Wow, man," she said.

"Do you see the fire?" I asked.

"Yeah, it's groovy!" she said.

She certainly didn't seem too alarmed by the flaming apocalypse overhead. "Hey, David," I said, "look up! The sky is on fire!"

I turned to look at David and Tina. Thankfully, they were not engaged in the throes of passion. Instead, they were already staring at the sky. "Yeah," Tina muttered dreamily. "It's a-may-zingggg."

I turned to Debbie, who had started playing with my hair and had a look of wonderment on her face. "Gabriel," she said, "you're on fire! Your white, white hair of light is on fire! It's beautiful!"

I felt my hair and was relieved to note that it was not, in fact, aflame. I looked deep into Debbie's eyes. Her pupils were huge! I checked out her hair, which did not appear to be burning at all, but then when I looked at the sky and back, it looked as though little sparks were flitting from the sky down to her and then back up again. I touched her head and laughed. Debbie was very pretty when she was sparking.

I tried to catch some of the sparks as they flew, but my hands seemed to be moving in slow motion. Debbie said, "You know what? I don't think those brownies were really brownies!"

Tina reached out and smacked her arm, which appeared to give off a shower of multicolored sparkles. "Yes, they were, silly! They must have been real brownies, because they were so brown and easy!"

This conversation was getting very hard for me to follow. "What-are-you-talking-about?" I asked.

Tina burst out laughing. "What-are-you-talking-about?" she said back to me. "I-am-talking-about-brown-easies!"

"But— but—" I stammered.

"Easy, brownie!" David said.

Debbie asked, "What was in these brown, brown brownies? David, do you know?" She broke off a chunk of the brownies and started poking through it. After what seemed like a million years, she held up a shriveled thing that might have been either a deformed, giant raisin or a dried-up slice of somebody's ear. "Aha!" she shouted. "What's this?"

David laughed. "Wow, happy birthday to me! I know what that is. I'll give you a hinty, minty hint: It's not chocolate. . . ."

Tina said, "That's a mushroom! We're all tripping on mushy, mushy mushrooms, aren't we?"

Holy cow, I thought. I tried really hard to concentrate on what this might mean. *Stay on the blanket,* I told myself. *Stay on the blanket. Michael wouldn't feed David anything he thought was dangerous, right? We just have to stay on the blanket and everything will be fine.*

Debbie's blissful face from moments before had been erased by a mask of near-panic. I attempted to conjure up the calmest voice I could, but when I spoke, the strangest thing happened: My words seemed to float out of me in a talk bubble, as though my life had been transformed into a comic book. I said, "Debbie, don't worry! We're together on this blanket of safety. Hold my hand. Okay? You are pretty. I like your sparky face and I am holding your hand."

She said, "You talk like the moon!"

Oddly, I felt at that moment like I knew exactly what she meant.

Time stretched and compacted; colors swirled and swooped everywhere I looked. I started to freak out several times, but whenever I did, I squeezed Debbie's hand and she squeezed back. Meanwhile, the next two bands, Canned Heat and Mountain, played their entire sets without me once looking in the direction of the stage.

I experienced the music, though. At certain moments, the whole universe seemed to be made of Jell-O, and each note rippled through the gelatinous worlds around me. At others, the notes were water, or electricity, or pure, frozen light. I tried to think about the chords, or the guitar fingerings I was hearing, but everything kept speeding up or slowing down so much that analysis was impossible. Trying to capture any kind of coherent thought was like trying to catch sand in a spaghetti strainer.

I didn't even notice when one band stopped and the next started.

At some point, though, Debbie suddenly crushed my hand super-hard. I sat upright and noticed three things:

1. The music had completely stopped.
2. It was pitch dark and raining.
3. Tina and David were gone.

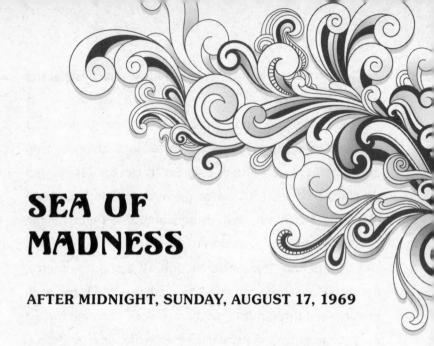

SEA OF MADNESS

AFTER MIDNIGHT, SUNDAY, AUGUST 17, 1969

I missed the Grateful Dead completely. I could have been the only guitar fan of my entire generation who got to see Jerry Garcia play live, but instead, I spent the next few hours running around in the dark, frantically screaming my father's name. Oh, I also met a couple of other rock stars, but ended my adventure in a hospital tent.

Kids, just say no to drugs. And/or brownies.

Debbie and I sat in the rain and looked around for what felt like a long time. Then she let go of my hand, stood up, and paced around the blankets. She even peeked into the tent—twice—before she straightened up and said, "Gabriel, I'm not sure, but I think Tina and David might be gone."

Duh.

Somehow, despite my wasted mental state, I remembered seeing a flashlight in one of the backpacks. I stood up and rummaged through two of the bags before finding it. I switched it on to make sure it worked, and Debbie said, "Wow, man, you brought a little sun! That's going to be really useful! We can just hold it up and then Tina and David can . . . What was I saying again? Hey, that light is really pretty!"

From the next blanket over, someone shouted, "Turn that thing off, man! You're ruining my trip!"

I issued the first of maybe a thousand apologies I would have to make during my hunt for my brother. Then I grabbed Debbie's hand and pulled her to her feet. "Come on," I said, "we have to find Tina and David!"

"Where are they?" she asked.

"I don't know! That's why we have to look for them."

"Oh, groovy!"

I took one step off the blanket and immediately stumbled over something on the ground. Pointing the flashlight straight down, I saw two pairs of incredibly muddy sneakers lined up side by side. Debbie bent way down and peered at the smaller pair. "Those are Tina's shoes," she said. "I was there when she got them. But she's not in them now."

You might notice that the mushrooms were doing wonders for our detection abilities.

"That's true," I said.

"I bet those are David's sneakers right . . . next . . . to . . . hers!"

"I bet you're right."

"And he's not in his, either!"

"That's also true."

"This . . . is . . . actually . . . good news," Debbie said. "Now all we have to do is follow their footprints!"

It seemed like a good idea, for about three seconds. We walked, and ran, and stumbled, and slipped all over the festival grounds, staring at the mud, each with one arm around the other's waist and one hand on our "little sun." Sometimes, I would forget what we were looking for and Debbie would remember. Other times she would be the one to forget. I even seem to remember a period in there where we both forgot what we were supposed to be doing, and sat down in a puddle for a while to watch people use the pay phones.

It probably doesn't sound that fascinating, but first of all, I've never used a pay phone. There are barely any left in the 2010s, but there were dozens of them all lined up in a row at Woodstock, and even in the middle of the rainy night, they were all getting used. Also, I imagined I could see the people's voices turning into multicolored lines of electricity, and then flying through the lines all over America. I asked Debbie whether she could see the voices too, and she answered with a hushed and awestruck "Yeeaaahhh . . ."

For a second, I wished I had my cell phone so I could make colors fly straight through the air without a wire, but then I thought, *No, you wouldn't have anyone to call, anyway. Because nobody else even has a cell phone.* That struck me as so hilarious that I started banging my head against Debbie's shoulder, laughing. She didn't even know what I was laughing about, but it didn't matter—she burst out, too.

When we finally got back under control, she said, "We should go to the stage and tell them we lost our friends. They can, like, announce it. That would be so groovy. We could even say it was David's birthday, and they could announce that, too!"

I sort of wanted to watch some more hot nonstop pay-phone action, but Debbie got me moving, and we made our way to the side of the stage. Some parts of what happened next are a blur, but I know we just kept marching up to people in Woodstock staff shirts and saying we really needed to see David and Tina. Of course, none of them paid any attention to two tripping fifteen-year-olds at first, but then I started telling everybody that I was friends with Jimi Hendrix.

That made them pay attention, because it made them think we were at least marginally psycho.

We got escorted, very gently, from the edge of the stage to a medical tent. A lady in a Woodstock security jacket handed us off to a tired-looking nurse. I think the security woman said something like, "We've got two more. This one here thinks he knows Hendrix!"

The nurse sat us down on the edge of a cot and started asking us questions about what we had taken. There was no way I was going to 'fess up to anything, so the conversation didn't go very smoothly:

Nurse: *Son, can you tell me what you're on?*
Me: *A cot.*
Nurse (sighing): *Can you tell me what you ingested?*
Me: *Brownies.*
Nurse: *What was in the brownies?*
Me: *Chocolate, flour, sugar . . . I don't know.*
Nurse: *You don't know?*
Me: *What do I look like, Betty Crocker?*

Debbie interrupted with a squeal: "Oh my gosh! That's John Sebastian from the Lovin' Spoonful!"

I turned away from the nurse, and saw that a couple of cots away, a guy was standing with an acoustic guitar, strumming and singing quietly to whomever was lying there. He was wearing glasses and a wildly tie-dyed jean jacket. I said, "THE John Sebastian? Who played onstage today?"

The nurse said, "No, the other John Sebastian that's walking around the festival with a guitar singing John Sebastian songs." Ouch. I guess I probably deserved that, but still . . .

Debbie said, "Wow, whoever's in that bed must be really important! Is it somebody famous, too?"

The nurse laughed. "No, honey, just two kids your age who came in about an hour ago. They were walking around in the dark barefoot—said they wanted to have 'an encounter with the Earth Goddess.' Instead, they had an encounter with some soda can tops. The doc just got done stitching 'em up, and now we're waiting to make sure they aren't having a reaction to the tetanus shots so they can get back to—hey, come back here!"

We ran over to the cot and had quite a joyous reunion. I know, I know: What are the chances that in a crowd of half a million people, we would all find each other in the dark, and then get a private concert from a rock star? All I can tell you is that in this case, the odds were 100 percent. My dad's left foot and Tina's right one were hugely bandaged, but they both had gigantic smiles on their faces as they listened to their new friend John singing a song he had done onstage that day called "Rainbows All Over Your Blues." After the first chorus, David and I even burst into three-part harmony, which I guess was pretty gutsy.

At the time, though, it felt perfect. It also looked awe

inspiring. I could see a stream of golden notes fluttering forth from David's mouth, intertwining with a river of reddish ones flowing from mine, and then mingling with a beautiful blue sea of words and chords coming from John and his guitar.

At the end of the song, John said, "Are you two friends with these two?" We all nodded in eerie unison, like trained seals. He grinned. "And I'm guessing you all shared dessert not too long ago?" We all nodded again, although I felt kind of sheepish, like I was getting busted. But he just grinned even wider and said, "Welcome to Woodstock, friends!"

Debbie said, "Um, Mr. Sebastian? Sir? Uh, your rock-star-ship?"

"Call me John."

"Your Johnship? How come you're playing here? I mean, it's really far out and all, but . . ."

"I've been playing here on and off all day, sweetheart. Mostly, I've been singing songs for kids who've been trying to come down off bad trips, you know? It really helps 'em to mellow out. You should have been here a few hours ago. Rick Danko from the Band was here jamming, too. It was a real sweet scene."

"That's amazing!" I said. I know you always hear about famous people stopping in at hospitals, hitting home runs for little Timmy with cancer and stuff like that, but when you're actually right there with the rock star, it's still kind of crazy.

David reached out and touched John's knee. "Hey, man. I just want to say thanks. The stitches kind of hurt, but it didn't bother me so much or anything with you here."

John smiled and said, "You're welcome."

Just then, a mousy-looking short woman with long, frizzy hair came rushing in, wearing a flowing, tie-dyed outfit and a million beads and bracelets. She was holding a lit cigarette and waving a bottle of Southern Comfort whiskey at John with the same hand. "Sebastian," she rasped, "I knew I'd find you here. Why isn't your scrawny Yankee ass backstage? Sly Stone is going crazy! He said you promised you'd check out his hair before he goes onstage, and he ain't leaving the trailer until you do!"

John grinned. "See ya, David. See ya, Tina. I guess that's my cue. Anyway, I'm starving. I gotta get something to eat from the hospitality area before Janis here eats all the bagels!"

"Awww!" Tina said.

"What's wrong?" John asked. I thought for sure Tina was going to beg him for an autograph, or bug him to take us backstage with him, or do something else that would totally ruin the moment.

Instead, her eyes literally filled with huge tears that

sparkled in the glaring, generator-fueled lights, and she said, "You're so nice. I'll miss you."

John Sebastian slung his guitar behind his back so it was out of the way, leaned down over the cot, and kissed Tina on the top of her head. Then he stood back up and froze for a moment, like he was pondering something really, really heavy.

Finally, he unfroze and said, "Hey, Janis? Do we have time for just one more song? Something to warm up your throat a little before your set?"

She took a huge pull on her cigarette and then gulped down a swig from her bottle. "Well, shit, 'Bastian. I have to sing for 'bout a million people tonight." She took a deep breath and wiped her mouth on the back of her sleeve. "So I guess it doesn't make any difference if I sing for a few more. Hey, why don't we try out that new song we were messing around with backstage?"

John started strumming on his guitar, and Janis's voice filled the tent: "Busted flat in Baton Rouge, waitin' for a train . . ."

———

After the song and a round of good-byes, Debbie, Tina, David, and I were left sitting on the cots in amazement, going, "Was that really—" "Did they really just—" "Did she—"

Then we would all burst out giggling.

The nurse must have gotten tired of watching this pattern repeat itself over and over, because eventually she said, "Yes, that was really Janis Joplin, and yes, she really sang a duet with the real John Sebastian, just for the four of you. Plus one lucky nurse."

We all smiled like fools. I had been pretty sure I wasn't completely hallucinating, and my trip seemed to be mostly over, but it was nice to hear some confirmation from someone who was sober. Unless, of course, I was imagining everything the nurse said, too.

"Anyway," she continued, "that was a nice ending to your weekend adventures, don't you think? In the morning, when the helicopters are flying again and we can get David and Tina out of here, they'll fly out with a great last memory of the concert."

BAD MOON RISING

I jumped up from the cot. "What?" I shouted. "You can't send them away before the concert's over!"

"Sure I can. They have deep, stitched-up wounds on their feet, no shoes, and miles of litter-strewn mud to cross in every direction. Do you want your friends' cuts to get infected?"

"N-no, but—"

"Listen, Junior, this is serious stuff. I'm an emergency room nurse. I've seen people lose legs because they didn't take care of injuries on their feet. This is a farm field—that means cows and horses, pigs, manure. You can't even imagine the nasty little bacteria that are swimming around in the muck out there."

"But—please. This is my friend's last chance to spend with his big brother before . . . um . . ."

"Before what?"

Geez. I couldn't exactly tell her. She wouldn't believe the word of a drugged fifteen-year-old, and even if she would, I couldn't say anything in front of David. "Nothing. It's just that this concert means a lot to my friend. Okay, what if I give him my shoes? I'll go barefoot back to our blankets, and then I'll put on his shoes there. Mine are cleaner, and we're the same size, anyway. It's just one more day, right? We have soap and everything. What if we promise we'll go to the pumps and wash his feet twice tomorrow?"

She stared me down with a tough-nurse glare. "Let me get this straight: You want to walk barefoot back on the same exact path that you know your friends just got cut up on?"

Well, when she put it that way it didn't sound terribly appealing, but I didn't see much choice. I gulped, crossed my fingers behind my back for luck, and nodded. "If you'll let us stay."

Debbie said, "Me, too. I'm the exact same size as Tina, and I would get cut for her any day. She'd do it for me in a heartbeat."

The nurse sighed. "This is crazy. If I weren't a volunteer, I'd get fired for this. Here's what I'm going to do. . . . We have a few pairs of sandals some kids left behind earlier today when they got choppered out of here. I'll give each of you a pair of sandals to wear so you don't get cut up, too. And I'm going to give your friends some penicillin pills to take. David and Tina, is either one of you allergic to antibiotics?"

They both shook their heads.

"Are you sure?"

They both shook them again.

"In that case, will each of you swear to me you'll take one of these every eight hours for the next ten days?"

They both nodded.

The nurse scurried over to a huge pile of cardboard boxes in the corner and started sorting through them, muttering, "Can't believe I'm doing this..." When she came back, she handed a pair of sandals each to Debbie and me, and a vial of pills each to David and Tina. Debbie and I gave our sneakers to our friends, who put them on gingerly and stood up very carefully.

As we all turned to leave, I said, "Is that it? Can we go now?"

The nurse said, "One more thing. Do you know my name?"

Tina frowned and said, "No, I don't think you ever told us."

The nurse smiled. "Excellent. Now get out of here. And try to have fun while you still have all your limbs!"

Walking through several inches of mud in oversize

sandals was an interesting experience, made even more so by the sounds of Creedence Clearwater Revival playing from the stage, the random flashes of psychedelic light that were still occasionally flashing across my vision, and Tina's cries of "Ouch!" every few steps.

"Should we go back and ask the nurse about the helicopter option?" Debbie asked her.

"No way, Deb! I am not missing Jimi Hendrix. He is the grooviest man alive!"

And I was running out of time to meet him.

David told us Michael and Willow would be frantically worried when we got back to the blankets, but actually they were unnaturally calm. We found them sitting perfectly still with their hands wrapped around their knees, watching the end of Creedence's set.

David knelt in front of his brother and said, "Michael, I'm so sorry! You told us to stay right here, but we ate the brownies, and then Tina saw these pretty lights floating through the air, so we decided to follow them, and, uh, I got a little spaced out for a while . . . and then some other stuff happened, and we ended up in this tent place, and we met John Sebastian and Janis Joplin. And oh yeah, I got some stitches in my foot. And a shot. But everything's cool, man. The nurse said I was good to go. Okay? Hello? Mikey? Are you mad? Aren't you speaking to me?"

Michael turned his head toward David in such super-slow

motion that he reminded me of a praying mantis, or some kind of gigantic, long-extinct plant-eating dinosaur. "You . . . met . . . Janis Joplin?" he asked. It looked as though formulating the question had taken a massive mental effort. "That's . . . groovy. Right, Willow?"

Willow gave us the same reptilian once-over and whispered, "Groovy. Come . . . sit with us."

At first I wasn't sure what was wrong with them. They weren't acting like anybody else I had talked to at Woodstock. It was almost like they had brain damage. Then I thought about what my father had said to me in the prison cell: *My brother died because of Woodstock.* And what my mother had said to me in our kitchen: *The boy had apparently been experimenting with heroin for two months or so.*

That was when I knew. My uncle Mike had just taken his first dose of heroin. Worse, he and Willow had tricked us. They had given us the mushroom brownies, knowing that we'd be too high for a few hours to do anything that would stop them from scoring.

And I still didn't understand why.

We all sat down, and David and the girls immediately launched into an extended retelling of our adventure. None of them seemed to notice that Michael and Willow were practically nodding out on their laps the whole time, but I did. Tears ran down my face, and I was glad for the dark. All I could think was, *Stupid, stupid, stupid. The guy has eight more Saturdays left on earth, and your only job was to stick with him and prevent this from happening. Instead, you got distracted by babes and brownies.*

Creedence launched into one of my all-time favorite songs, "Bad Moon Rising," and a chill shot through me. I thought, *I love this band, I love this song, and I will never want to hear either of them again as long as I live.*

I lay on my side for a while, turned away from everybody else, and tried really hard to think of something useful to say or do. But I was incredibly tired, my uncle had just done exactly what I had hoped to stop him from doing, and I still hadn't even come close to meeting Jimi Hendrix. Nothing was working, and friendly, cheerful David was going to grow up and turn into the exact same bitter father I had always known.

At some point, I must have started to doze off, but a hand on my shoulder jolted me awake. I sat upright, and my face banged into Willow's. "Hey, sleeping angel Gabriel," she slurred, "you'll miss Janisssss."

How could they all sit around talking like nothing was wrong? That was the craziest thing about Woodstock, I guess: The drugs really did seem like a good idea at the time. Everyone was having fun, right? I had seen and heard enough to know how protective Michael was of David, but he had thought nothing of getting David wasted and then leaving him in a field amid half a million drugged-up strangers. And, hey, for most of these people, most of the time, on any given drug trip everything would turn out all right. As far as I could remember, only one person at the whole festival had died of an overdose.

I got another chill. I was pretty sure the guy had died on Saturday night, from heroin. For all I knew, he was dying, somewhere out there in the darkness, at that exact moment.

Anyway, over time, a lot of these people's lives were going to be absolutely wrecked by drugs and alcohol. They didn't know it, but I sure did. I thought about the bands at Woodstock. The toll was going to be devastating:

- Multiple members of Canned Heat; Tim Hardin; Janis Joplin; two members of the Who; and of course, Jimi Hendrix would all die young from overdoses or drug- and alcohol-related misadventures.
- Sly Stone; various members of the Crosby, Stills, Nash, and Young band; the lead singer of the Grateful Dead; and Johnny Winter, among others, would go through years of substance abuse and mess up their lives and careers.

And, of course, there were several people on this very blanket whose futures were being demolished as we spoke.

I sat up and wiped my eyes. "Willow, are you feeling all right?" I asked.

"I feel sssuper-greaterrific," she said.

I did not find that comforting.

"Hey, Gabriel, thanks for bringing my little brother back, man," Michael said. It was so dark now that I couldn't really see anybody, but he still sounded just about as spacey as Willow did.

"I didn't really do anything. Debbie and I just walked around until we accidentally found David and Tina. It was no big deal."

Tina said, "It was a big deal. You gave us your shoes. If not for you two, I wouldn't even be here right now. I would have had to stay in that tent. I would have missed Jimi Hendrix!"

I said, "But we had to give you our shoes. I mean, I couldn't have come back here without David. He's my ride home, right? And I don't want to leave early, either. So, uh, it's not like I was being some big hero or something. And neither was Debbie."

Suddenly, an elbow jabbed into my ribs. "Hey, I resent that! I happen to think I am an excellent hero. Heroine. Hero-ish type of person," Debbie said. Then she added, "Okay, I'm kidding. He's right. We didn't do anything any of you wouldn't have done. And it wasn't heroic, either. It was kind of selfish, if you really think about it. Tina has my

159

bus ticket, so I have to stick with her. If I didn't want to leave early, I had to fork over my shoes."

Tina said, "God, Debbie. You are a selfish bitch!" Then she burst out laughing.

David spoke next, and something in his tone raised the hair on the back of my neck. "Gabriel, you're honest. I don't think I've ever really met anybody honest before. Most people try to take credit for things, whether they deserve it or not. But I think you're nicer than you think you are. You didn't have to come looking for me. You could have just stayed here and, uh, played with Debbie."

Willow said, "Wait a minute, Davey. Mikey is always honest with you."

"No, he's not. He protects me. You both do, and I appreciate it. But that's not the same as telling me the truth. Anyway, thanks, Gabriel. That's all I'm trying to say."

My eyes welled up. I hadn't been honest. I hadn't been honest with any of these people, although I was trying really hard to be kind and unselfish. As Janis Joplin came onstage and her band fired up their first song, I realized I couldn't remember the last time my father had thanked me sincerely for helping him unselfishly. In fact, as hard as I tried, I couldn't remember a time I had helped him unselfishly.

I racked my brain until my head hurt, but I came up blank all around.

UNCLE SAM BLUES

SUNDAY, AUGUST 17, 1969

"**D**avid was right. You are honest. That's why we have to have this talk."

It was maybe four in the morning, and somewhere far in the distance behind us, Sly and the Family Stone were playing "Dance to the Music"—you know, that epic song from the end of *Shrek*. The crowd was absolutely roaring, and I kind of wished I could be back on the blankets, snuggled up with Debbie. Even in the middle of this insane situation, things had been getting intense with her a few songs ago. Then, out of the blue, Willow had started poking me and giggling.

"Come on, Lover Angel Boy! Michael and Willow need you for a little while. It's Walking Time!"

Believe me, those had not been welcome words, and Debbie had tried to get me to stay. In fact, she had been extremely convincing.

And yet, here I was, stumbling along in the pitch blackness with Michael's arm draped over one shoulder and Willow's over the other. We had told Debbie, David, and Tina we would be back soon, and then found our way out to the main path we had followed into the concert. Now I was pretty sure the woods were on our right, and we were heading over the hill toward the highway.

"What are we doing?" I asked.

Willow said, "I'm sorry, Gabey. I know you were having all kinds of fun back there. But this is important. Mikey needs to tell you something. Something Davey is not allowed to know."

Michael yanked us all off to the right, into the trees. We went crashing through underbrush for maybe thirty feet, and then he stopped short. My eyes had adjusted to the darkness just enough that I could see we were in a little clearing. I could also see that we were all alone.

It felt strange to be in such a secluded place after being packed in among hundreds of thousands of screaming rock fans all weekend. The music seemed a million miles away. Michael whispered, "Sit down."

Willow whispered back, "Aye, aye."

I said, "Why are you talking like a pirate, Willow?"

Willow said, "I don't know. Why is Mikey whispering?"

I said, "This is really serious, isn't it, Michael?"

Michael said, "Yessss, but . . . it's all groovy now, man. Everything is going to work out fine. You just have to swear on your life you won't tell my brother what I am about to tell you."

"Until when?"

Michael sucked in his breath so sharply it whistled through his teeth. "For as long as I'm alive. Or my father. You have to swear that as long as my father is alive, or I am, you won't tell David my secret."

"All right, Michael. I swear on my life. You can trust me with your secret. Now what is it? I need to know."

"It's the letter, man. Uncle Sam wants me. I got drafted. I'm supposed to go to Vietnam. Ain't that a bitch?"

Vietnam. Of course. That explained everything—why Michael had suddenly gotten so touchy when his brother had mentioned the war, why he had been treating this like some special last big weekend, and why he didn't want David to know. David would be *destroyed* by this.

"So," I said, "what are you going to do?"

"Well, I'll tell you what I'm not going to do. I'm not going to fight in this old man's war. First of all, I don't believe in it, and second, I can't leave David in my parents' house without me around to look after him. I mean, sometimes they don't even feed the kid—and that's when I am here."

"So, uh, you could go to Canada, right? Or you could tell the government you don't want to shoot anybody. You could be a—what's it called—a—"

"Conscientious objector. Nope, I can't do either of those."

"Why not?"

Michael sighed. Willow put her arm around him, cradled his head to her breast, and said, "His dad, Gabey. The old man fought in France in the Second World War. Came home completely ruined in the head, you know? But don't let Mr. Barber hear you say that. Anyway, one night, right after the letter came, Michael said something like, 'What would you think if I got drafted and became a conscientious objector?' His dad had had a few drinks, right? And he looked Mikey right in the eye and said, 'I'd rather be the father of a dead soldier than a live coward.' "

"God," I said. "That's awful."

"Yeah," Michael slurred.

"But wait! Why don't you apply to college? Don't college students get excused from the draft?"

"I coulda done that. I coulda. But Dad always said he only had one son who wasn't too much of a dumbass for college—and I wasn't the one. Anyway, doesn't matter. It's all fine."

He suddenly sounded cheery again. It was pretty hard

to keep up with the mood swings with this crowd. "Everything's going to be fine. I've got this all worked out now. We don't have to worry anymore. Okay? Okay. I'm glad we have this settled. I jus' wanted you to know about the letter, that's all."

He started to stand back up, but I grabbed his arm.

"Wait a minute," I said. "How is this settled? You just said you can't run away, and you can't be a conscientious objector. So how is this all supposed to work out, exactly? I don't understand."

"I have a plan, Gabriel. A top-secret plan. I went into the forest and bought some stuff—some H—tonight. See, I have to pass a physical exam for the army in October. But I'm going to use some of this stuff . . . and . . . and . . . um . . ." He trailed off.

Willow looked up from stroking Michael's hair and said, "And the army is going to think he's a druggie hippie freak, so he's going to fail his physical! Then they'll let him out of the army. And we can get married, and make babies, and bake bread, and live on a farm out in the country. And we'll take Davey with us, and Mikey's parents will never bother us again and . . . Mikey? Mikey?"

Michael had nodded off in Willow's lap.

"Heroin?" I asked her. She nodded. "Willow, that's bad stuff. You have to believe me. I know you both think this is the only way, but it isn't. So what if Michael's father gets mad at him for a while? Isn't Mr. Barber an insane drunk anyway?"

"Aww, Gabey, don't you know? Mikey still loves his dad. You don't get to choose who you love in this world, sweetheart."

"But heroin. Heroin. He could become an addict. You could become an addict. Look at you. You're so beautiful." I felt myself blushing, even in the cold darkness. "I mean, heroin makes people so skinny and ugly and—"

She still had Michael in her lap, but she somehow freed up one arm and put it around my shoulder. I felt her breath against my throat. "You really are the sweetest angel." My blush got about ten degrees hotter. So did the rest of me. "But it's okay. We asked around about this. You only get addicted if you shoot the stuff into your veins. And it takes a while. We just snorted it into our noses to see what it was like. Plus, I'm not even going to do it again. We have to save the rest for Mikey's plan. I'll still stay beautiful for you." She did her famous giggle thing again.

Of all the inappropriate times to be on fire with desire, this had to take the freaking grand prize.

"Uh," I stammered, "I'm pretty sure you're wrong about the addiction thing. You can get addicted just from snorting. And it can happen really, really fast."

Willow was laughing silently. "Wow," she murmured, "angels sure do worry a lot."

"And, um, by the way, why can't I tell David about the letter?"

Willow started stroking my hair with one hand while she was still playing with Michael's with the other. I had heard about the whole 1960s free love thing, but this was ridiculous. "You'll have to ask Mikey about that one in the morning, Gabey. But basically, it's their dad again. Mikey always hides plans from Davey, for Davey's own good. David can't know about any of this, because when Mr. Barber finds out that David knew about a secret before he did, he flips out. And then the punishment is bad, man. Really bad. If David finds out that Mikey dodged the draft— and then their dad finds out later? Oh, God. I don't even want to think about that scene."

We sat in silence for a while, and I gradually became aware that the music had stopped. I didn't want to move or say anything, partly because I had so much to think about, partly because I was the most exhausted I had ever been in my life, and partly because Willow was still playing with my hair. I know it might sound odd to say that each hair root on my head was individually sending little personal messages of joy and celebration to my brain, but it's also the truth. I was going crazy in several different ways.

Then, at the very edge of our hearing, the concert started up again with an explosion of drums. Willow gasped and yanked me and Michael to our feet. "Oh, we have to get back there!" she practically shouted. "I know this song! It's the Who! Michael, wake up, honey! It's the Who! They're playing 'Heaven and Hell!'"

Well, that's appropriate, I thought.

She turned to me. "Mikey loves the Who! Come on!"

Before I could even process the sad fact that Willow's fingers were no longer in contact with my scalp, we were crashing through the underbrush.

It must have taken us twenty minutes to find our way back to our group, and I was amazed when we did. Again, the sound mixing station was what guided us in.

When we were maybe ten feet away from the blankets, approaching from behind, Willow pushed Michael ahead. Then she said to me, "I'm sorry I interrupted you and your girlfriend before, angel Gabriel."

"Uh, it's okay, I guess. I mean, this was important, right? And, uh, I mean—"

"Shhh," she said, and put a finger on my lips. "I think you still have an hour or so before it gets light."

"Nah," I said, her finger tickling against my nose as I spoke, "Debbie's probably asleep by now. Besides, after all that heavy stuff, I'm not really in the mood anymore. I think I'll just sit on the blanket and listen to the music. Really, it's okay. I don't need to—"

Willow said, "You're not in the mood anymore? Really? What a waste. You're a fifteen-year-old boy. Get in the mood!" Then she hugged me very, very close, and sort of ground herself against me for thirty seconds or so.

It worked.

"Now go get that girl," Willow said.

Tired, half-crazy, and confused as I have ever, ever been, I did.

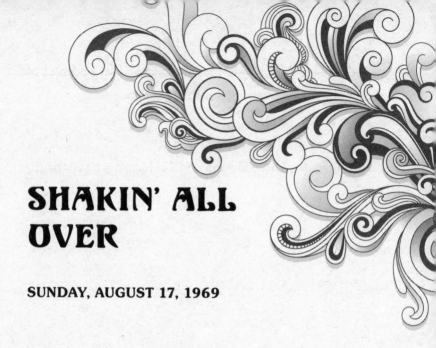

SHAKIN' ALL OVER

SUNDAY, AUGUST 17, 1969

I woke up for a little while when a stage announcer said, "What we have in mind is breakfast in bed for four hundred thousand!" Then I turned over, put my bare arm over Debbie's, and tried to fall asleep again. The next thing I knew, some random dude in a buckskin jacket was actually holding a cup of granola in my face. I took the cup, just to make him go away, and turned over again.

Debbie and I slept through the Jefferson Airplane's early-morning set, and for several hours after that. I only woke up for good when David shook my foot, handed me a cup of lukewarm tea, and said, "Gabriel, I need help. There's something wrong with my brother!"

I sat up. The first thing I noticed was that I wasn't

wearing a shirt, and that my hood-ornament bruise was turning a sick shade of green. The second thing was that I was starving. I said, "What do you mean?"

While David composed his thoughts, I fumbled around on the muddy, rumpled blanket for that cup of granola and started gulping it down with the tea. Then I said, "Wait! Is this tea safe? Where did you—"

He said, "There's nothing wrong with the tea. A bunch of nuns came around with tea and sandwiches about fifteen minutes ago. I don't think nuns are going to spike anybody's drink, all right? So I got my brother a cup of tea, because he loves caffeine in the morning. And I stuck my head in the tent, and Michael and Willow were both kind of asleep, but they were groaning. I shook Willow's foot, and she didn't want to wake up, but she did. Then I shook my brother's foot, and he won't wake up. He won't wake up!"

I swallowed the rest of my tea in one chug, got up, and looked around. The whole area looked like a refugee camp. There was mud and trash everywhere, and the few people who were walking around all looked as stunned as I felt. I stepped over to the tent and knelt down to look through the flap. Willow was holding Michael's hand and murmuring to him. She looked relieved when she saw us.

"Gabriel, David, can you boys help me get him sitting up? I think if I can just get him upright, he'll come around."

Her voice, which had sounded so flirty and playful last night, was high and shaky.

We squeezed our upper bodies into the opening and each managed to get an arm beneath Michael's shoulders. Willow counted to three, and we lifted Michael until his head was nearly vertical. Then his eyes popped open and he grabbed his stomach. "I have to—" he said, and staggered to his feet.

He made it out of the tent before the vomiting started, but unfortunately, he didn't make it to the edge of the blankets.

That made it Tina's second consecutive morning of waking up covered in barf. I had always heard New York City girls were good at cursing, but truly, I had no idea. The scope, power, and precision of Tina's vocabulary were simply beyond words. Or at least they were beyond the kind of words a Pennsylvania boy like me would know how to use with any fluency.

Debbie jumped up, grabbed her bag, and hurried Tina off in the direction of the water pumps. Meanwhile, David grabbed his brother, a bottle of shampoo, and the blanket, and headed down toward the pond. That left me and Willow standing on the other blanket, staring around at nothing.

"Wow," I said. "Good morning."

She hugged herself and shivered. "Gabriel," she said,

"is there another cup of that tea? And are you cold? I'm cold."

Willow sat down. I realized David had lined up four cups of tea next to the tent. Score another two points for my father: As a teenager, he had been really considerate. And an early riser.

I sat down next to her and handed her one of the paper cups. She took it in both hands and said, "You were right, Gabriel. That . . . stuff . . . last night was awful. I'm scared. Look at my hands." I looked, and saw that her arms were shaking so badly that the tea was sloshing around almost to the rim of the cup. When she took a sip, some of the liquid even spilled down her chin.

"God," she said, "this is terrible. Do you know what the worst part is?"

I didn't say anything. Honestly, what was I supposed to say?

Willow stared into my eyes, and for a moment I could have sworn she looked a thousand years old. "Gabriel, the worst part is, my first thought when I woke up was . . . I want MORE. How sick is that?"

I said, "You can't do any more. You can't touch any more heroin. He can't, either. It's a matter of life and death. I'm serious."

She put down her tea and reached out to squeeze my right hand. Then she gave me that thousand-yard stare again, and said, "That's what you were sent here to tell us, isn't it?"

I swallowed. I was pretty sure this was one of those "DON'T RUIN THE SPACE-TIME CONTINUUM" moments. I said, "Listen, Willow, you don't need to be some kind of magical angel to realize heroin is bad news. Do you?"

She smiled. For the most beautiful, tanned hippie girl in the universe, who had been outdoors all weekend, she looked incredibly pale in the morning light, but at least she was smiling. "No," she half-whispered. "I guess you don't."

When everybody got back, Michael looked tired, but basically all right. He asked for a cup of tea and sat down on the other side of Willow to sip it. His hands didn't look shaky at all. In fact, as soon as he finished, he asked me to bring him his guitar from the tent. I had forgotten all about the guitar in the madness of the weekend, but as soon as I opened its case, I gasped.

Michael noticed. "You like it?" he asked. "It's a Martin. I think they're the only serious choice if you're going to play popular music." If the hair on my neck kept standing at attention like this, I was afraid it would eventually just stay up in a permanent neck-Mohawk. Michael's guitar was exactly the same left-handed model my father would buy me one day.

"Wow," I said. "It's gorgeous."

He flashed a grin, and it was as though he hadn't been in a near-coma fifteen minutes before. "My baby," he said. Then he started strumming.

Debbie came over and stood over me. I instantly became aware that I hadn't brushed my teeth or anything, which made me feel pretty darn awkward about the whole morning-after greeting. I was fairly sure that if we kissed, she would keel over and gag. I told her I really needed to freshen up, grabbed David's toothpaste and soap, and hustled away to the pumps. Behind me, I thought I heard Tina ask, "What's his problem?"

All I could think was, *Good lord, did I really just say "freshen up?" What am I, seventy?*

There was a huge line for water and an even longer one for the Porta Potties, so by the time I was all ready to face my day, I had apparently missed the beginning of a pretty major hippie sing-along back at what was left of our blanket area. Michael was playing guitar, and he and David were harmonizing. They were singing some pop tunes, and a crowd of maybe twenty-five people had gathered around.

My father and uncle sounded great! They did a Bob Dylan song, followed by two Simon and Garfunkel songs and one Beatles tune. I edged my way through the crowd in time to sing harmonies on the Beatles song, and then Michael held the guitar out to me. "Wanna play one, Gabriel? I'm a little wiped out!"

I tried to pass, but everybody started encouraging me, and Debbie pushed me forward. So I strapped on my uncle's Martin, our little circle cheered, and I became the only performer at Woodstock who hadn't even been born yet. David, Michael, and I did a few Bob Dylan songs, then finished up with "I'm a Believer" by the Monkees—which was another song I only knew because of the *Shrek* movie. But hey, it went over incredibly well.

As soon as I handed the Martin back to my uncle, I walked over to Debbie and attempted to apologize for running away to brush my teeth. However, she threw her arms around me and gave me one of her ambush kisses, so I guessed the apology could wait.

Guitars: get yourself one.

Anyway, the morning and the beginning of the afternoon were really mellow and nice. Any awkwardness with Debbie seemed to have been swept away by the kiss, Michael and Willow had perked up after the tea and guitar-playing, and we had enough granola and nun-made PB&J sandwiches to get us through our various hangover-type problems. Sometime after lunch, things started to get weird. First, the helicopter traffic picked up. Choppers had been flying around and landing backstage all weekend, carrying supplies, ferrying musicians and equipment, and even air-lifting medical casualties out, but it was only annoyingly loud when there wasn't a band playing. Suddenly, our quiet conversations turned into mini-shouting matches just so we could hear each other. Also, some of the helicopters had U.S. Army markings, and Michael's mood definitely seemed to grow darker whenever one of those flew over.

The stage announcements became much more frequent as the concert started gearing up for the day, which meant another source of commotion. I was getting nervous, because this was the start of the last day of the concert, and I still hadn't met Jimi Hendrix. Plus, Michael had used heroin. Sure, I had done some really fun stuff, heard some legendary musicians play, and met an awesome girl I would never see again, but if I had to grade this mission on its success so far, it would have to be a *Fail* all the way.

At some point, Tina convinced Debbie they should go down to the water and wash their hair. David was pretty excited to join them, but somehow visiting that scene with my dad and two girls in broad daylight was just too weird for me, so I stayed back.

Which left me alone with Willow and Michael. As soon as his brother was out of sight, Michael sort of deflated. He leaned sideways against Willow and said, "Jesus, I couldn't fake it anymore. I feel like I'm going to cry."

She just stroked his hair, until finally he continued. "I don't know what I was thinking. There's no way my plan is going to work. It's stupid. My father will find out I've been drafted. Or David will. Or my parents will find my stash.

Or—God!—I'll get strung out on the heroin, and then pass the physical anyway."

Michael was right. Unless something pretty amazing happened in the next twenty hours or so, his plan was going to end his life, ruin his brother's, and overshadow the first fifteen years of mine.

SOMETHING'S COMING ON

SUNDAY, AUGUST 17, 1969

When the roadies started setting up the drums and amps for the first band of the day, I had an idea: Maybe I should ask around and find out whether Hendrix was backstage yet. Even though it hadn't helped at all the night before when we were high, it seemed like maybe I might be able to be a bit slicker about the whole thing when I had my wits about me.

As soon as Debbie got back, I asked if she was up for a walk, and we made our way to the fencing by the left side of the stage area. It was a lot easier in daylight. It was simple enough to find a little cluster of Woodstock employees, and Debbie asked a guy whether Jimi Hendrix had arrived yet. The dude started into a whole "I wish we could tell you that, but it's classified" speech, which was what I had sort of figured would happen.

Just then, I caught a glimpse of John Sebastian walking by between slats of the tall fence that separated us from the backstage area. "John! Mr. Sebastian!" I yelled. "It's Gabriel, from last night in the medical tent! You sang to us?" He glanced over, but I could tell it wasn't clicking.

Debbie added, "With Janis Joplin?"

That did it. John Sebastian's face opened up into a huge grin, and he strode right up to a break between the slats. "Hey, guys," he said. "What's going on? How are your friends' feet doin' today?"

"They're fine," I said. "Did Janis eat all the bagels?"

He laughed. "Yup. But it was all okay, because the guys from Mountain brought a whole bunch of barbecued chickens. Chickens—can you believe it? Anyway, what are you doing over here, getting hassled by security?"

One of the Woodstock dudes sputtered, "We weren't hassling—"

John laughed again, and said, "I know, I know. I was just kidding. But seriously, man. What are you kids up to? I know a hustle when I see one, and you're definitely hustling."

"Well, um, I was just trying to find out whether Jimi Hendrix was here yet."

"You and about half a million other people, my friend."

"I know, but . . . it's really important. I can't tell you

why, but I think my friend—the one from last night? I think my friend and his brother really have to meet him."

"Listen, Gabriel. Gabriel, right?"

I nodded.

"I'm really tired, man, and I have to go crash for a while. But I'll tell you this. Jimi's a friend of mine, and he hasn't gotten here yet, as far as I know. Now here's what I'll do. I'll write down your name on a piece of paper, and later on, when I wake up, if Jimi is willing to see you and your friends, I'll have Chip—you know, the announcer?—call you to the stage. All right?"

"Really? You'd do that?"

"I already played a private concert for you, didn't I?" He smiled. I swear, John Sebastian was like Santa Claus with a guitar. "But I'm not promising anything. I mean, everybody wants to meet Jimi. And sometimes Jimi just wants some hang time, you know?"

"Okay," Debbie said. "We understand."

"Wow, thanks, Mr. Sebastian!" I shouted, as he started walking away. He waved over one shoulder.

"Well, that was pretty amazing," a female Woodstock crew member said to us. "Most of the performers aren't that nice."

One of the male crew members snickered and said, "You got that right. Last night, I saw Keith Moon spit on a kid who reached out to touch his arm through the fence."

I asked the Woodstock people, "Do you think he'll remember to write my name down? And do you think Jimi Hendrix will really get them to call us backstage?"

All of a sudden, none of them wanted to make eye contact with me. That pretty much gave me the answer I had expected. Debbie and I headed back toward the others.

Debbie said, "That might work, right? I know it might not, but at least it might."

I said, "Yeah."

"Gabriel," she asked, "why is meeting Jimi so important to you?"

I stopped walking. "I'm sorry, Deb, but I can't tell you. It's just . . . I kind of have a reason why I had to come this weekend, and I think getting David, Michael, and Jimi Hendrix together is part of what I have to do."

She turned to me, took both of my hands in hers, and said, "You know that sounds totally insane, right?"

Feeling myself blushing, I nodded.

"But I believe you. I guess that makes me crazy, too. Either that, or those were some seriously long-acting brownies." She pulled me close and kissed me softly. Then she kind of pushed me back so we were looking into each other's eyes at arm's length. "We're not going to see each other again, are we?" Wow, this was a new twist: a kissing ambush, with a devastating emotional question attached.

I looked at her for the longest time. I thought of a

million things to say, but every single one of them made me a lying player to one extent or another. I could lie outright, and be all *Sure, baby, I'll call you*, just to make our last night together buttery smooth. I could make up some half-truth, like *I'll be thinking of you*, or *We'll see what happens*, or that old online favorite, *It's complicated*.

I suppose I waited too long, because she half-turned away and said, "You know, my dad's a lawyer, and he always says you should never ask a witness a question unless you're a hundred percent sure you want the whole courtroom to hear the answer."

She bit her lip, looked at me again, and continued. "But it's okay, Gabriel. I mean, Tina and I kind of made a plan before this weekend. We have some boys that we sometimes date at home, you know? Nothing serious or anything, just dates. And Tina told me on the bus, 'Let's just forget about everybody we know for a few days, all right? I want to pretend that this concert is a little magical bubble of time, and everything we do in this bubble is going to be different—and magical—and beautiful—and separate from the regular world.' "

She leaned in and kissed me, on the cheek this time. "Gabriel . . . Gabriel, whose last name I will never even know. Gabriel . . . you will always be the honest, noble boy who escorted me through my magical bubble of time. How does that sound?"

I swallowed. Then I let go of Debbie's hands so I could put my fingers beneath her chin and tilt her face up to mine, and kissed her as slowly and gently as I knew how. "It sounds perfect."

We held hands all the way back to the blankets. Just before we arrived, I said, "Wow, who knew Tina was so smart?" But as soon as our little group was in sight, I felt like taking back the question, because Tina and David were enjoying the last few crumbs of an early dinner feast: the last of the mushroom brownies.

"Oh, you didn't!" Debbie said.

"Oh, we did!" Tina giggled. "C'mon, it's our last night together, Deb!"

"It's, like, two in the afternoon, Tina."

"So, okay, the night is young. But still—"

Michael and Willow were sitting facing them, smoking a joint, eating crackers, and smiling. Willow said, "Hey, we figured they might as well eat up. No sense in bringing anything home, right?"

Oh, you're bringing something home, I thought. *Something illegal that starts with an "H." I just wish you weren't.*

Debbie sighed and sat down next to Willow. "Oh, what the hell," she said. "Would you mind passing that joint over here?"

Willow gave her a quick, sisterly half hug and said, "Hey, I thought you'd never ask."

By the time Joe Cocker's band started playing, everybody but me was rolling. There were a couple of instrumentals, and then the Woodstock crowd got its first taste of the lead singer's shockingly powerful growl. I still had the ominous feeling that had been building in me for hours, and the very air around us was starting to taste coppery like it sometimes does before a thunderstorm—but David and Tina were up and swaying in each other's arms, Michael was yanking Willow to her feet, and before I could say no, Debbie had me moving, too.

The first few songs were mostly slow burners and medium-tempo boogies, and the huge crowd slowly fell into a groove. During the third, a sad tune called "Do I Still Figure in Your Life?" I actually started getting pretty melancholy thinking about everything that only I knew was going to be lost so soon, but then the next song, "Feelin' Alright," was a much faster, Latin-sounding kind of dance thing that got Debbie bouncing against me. I forgot to think for a while after that.

A couple of songs later, Joe Cocker burst into something called "Let's Go Get Stoned"—and the entire crowd became his personal half-million-buddy entourage. People were screaming, yelling, dancing naked. It was crazy. I looked around at the scene and thought, *Wow, just when you think Woodstock has stopped surprising you . . .*

We listened, and danced, and made out. Even though

Debbie deserved all of my attention, I stole little glances around at the crowd, partly because I had a strange feeling David might disappear again, and partly because I felt like the sky was getting darker and darker. When Joe Cocker started playing his last song, the Beatles' "With a Little Help from My Friends," the double storm finally hit.

The song was amazing. I am a huge Beatles fan, but I swear to you, Joe Cocker did it better than they did. Check it out online if you don't believe me. Anyway, somehow we all ended up with our arms linked. So did tens of thousands of people all around us in every direction. It was the hugest manifestation yet of the Woodstock uni-mind.

One thing about being the only un-high person in a group is that everyone else is living exactly in the moment, and you are basically the only one worrying about the past or the future. I was thinking about the words of the song, and how the Beatles were breaking up right at that moment, even though nobody at the concert really knew it yet. So the song was kind of a lie already. Looking down the line, I noticed that David and Michael had one arm over each other, and the other over their dates. I started wondering whether Michael was David's only friend. I mean, it would be really sad if your big brother was your only friend, even in a normal situation, but knowing what I knew made the whole thing just unbearable.

And geez, it might be true. Debbie was here with Tina.

Michael had Willow. But David had tagged along because Michael was the one person in the world he most wanted to spend time with. And David hadn't mentioned any actual friends all weekend. I mean, neither had I, but I knew I had some back home—I just couldn't talk too much about my life at all. And maybe he was just so caught up in Tina, and the music, and his brownie tripping, that he hadn't had time to make a big speech about his old pals back in Bethlehem, Pennsylvania—but, come to think of it, he had never really talked to me about any childhood friends in my "real" life, either. He must have spent a lot of time with the other guys in the band, but from what I understood, they were really Michael's friends, and our family definitely hadn't heard from any of them since I had been old enough to notice.

It was amazing my father had managed to hold it together into adulthood at all.

I broke our little dance line and dragged Debbie over behind David and Michael, just in time to notice two things. First, both my father and my uncle appeared to be staggering a bit. Second, Michael was shouting mushy sweet nothings in David's ear.

Just as the song's volume died down into the famous bridge ("Would you believe in a love at first sight?"), Michael asked, "Davey, what would you think if I had to, um, go away for a while?"

Oh, shit, really? I thought. Clearly, male bonding was yet another of the things that should never, ever mix with drugs.

The song went on for another couple of massively triumphant minutes as the audience howled into the sky, gigantic thunderheads massed above us, and Michael gradually grew to understand that his baby brother was working frantically to break his grip and run away into the crowd.

I WANT TO TAKE YOU HIGHER

SUNDAY, AUGUST 17, 1969

The instant the song ended, some guy onstage told Joe Cocker, "Look behind you! The weather!" The storm blew in like something out of biblical times. All weekend long, some brave audience members had been climbing up on the huge sixty-foot-tall metal lighting towers to get a better view of the stage, and now the official announcer, that Chip guy, started asking them to get down before the wind and the lightning made things really alarming up there.

Somehow, the repeated announcements must have penetrated David's drug-and-emotion-induced fog, because he ripped himself away from Michael and darted off in the direction of the nearest tower. Willow, who had been watching the strange arm-jostling scene, said, "Michael, I think he's going to climb up that metal thing!"

Now, I have to say, if I had been Michael, I don't care how super-hot Willow is. I would have been completely incapable of stopping myself from blurting out, *No shit!*

But to Michael's credit, he didn't. Instead, he gritted out, "Looks that way. But he can't be that stupid. Can he?"

Willow said, "Oh, Mikey. He's not stupid. He's hurting. Go!"

Michael went. As the rains came, and the lightning began, I followed. Pushing through the thick crowd and the slippery mud with near-zero visibility was slow going, so we couldn't have been more than thirty or so feet behind David, and we were both shouting his name the whole way. But between the sounds of the rain, the thunder, and the gusting winds, plus the noise of all the people, there was no way David was going to hear us—even if he would have been inclined to listen.

Halfway to the tower, I slipped on somebody's abandoned sleeping bag, and tumbled down a little hill. By the time I recovered and wiped the muck off my face, I couldn't see my father, or even my uncle. I sprinted for the tower. When I got there, Michael was leaning against the bottom, holding his ribs, winded. It was pretty hard to see anything clearly, but it looked to me as though one whole side of his body was covered in mud.

As soon as I slid to a stop, he said, "David pushed me. He actually pushed me!"

"Where is he?" I asked.

Michael pointed straight up.

I looked, and my head spun. My father was at least forty feet up in the air, suspended on the crisscrossed metal rigging of the lighting tower to the left of the stage. The wind was whipping up at forty or fifty miles an hour, and even where I was on the ground, that was enough to make my feet slip and slide in the muck. There was no way he was having an easy time hanging on to wet metal, especially not in his current mental state.

I had to shout to be heard over the gusting wind. "Michael, how are we supposed to get him down?"

"Easy," he said. "We go up!"

Of course, it would have to be at that exact moment that the first jagged bolt of lightning slashed across the blackening sky. Onstage, the announcer was telling everyone it was their last chance to get down from the towers, and looking up, I could see that even the Woodstock crew guys were scurrying down away from the lights as fast as they could. It looked like what happens when you pour boiling water on an anthill—but one crazy ant was still going in the wrong direction.

In the light of the next flash, Michael looked haggard. "Forget it, Gabriel!" he yelled. "You go back to the blankets and stick with Willow. I don't want you to get turned into an angel for real!"

"What about you?"

"Come on, man. He's my baby brother. Now go. I gotta get up there."

Michael started climbing, and my mind turned over and over. *You might as well let him go up alone, I thought. You know he's not supposed to die today, right? Plus, you know your father makes it through this. The only person who might be in real danger up there would be you.*

But then, as I looked up at David way above my head, and Michael slowly ascending, I realized things might be much worse than I'd thought:

It's one-on-one, and Michael is the one person in the world David doesn't want to listen to right now. That's no good. If my coming back here has already changed everything—if all of this might make a difference—then my father and my uncle could both be in danger now, too.

All bets are off.

I reached up and grabbed the lowest rung of the scaffolding. I had thought the storm was already at its worst, but I had been wrong. When I was maybe twenty feet up, the wind hit another level completely, and the rain started blowing sideways directly into my eyes. I could feel the biggest gusts tugging at my T-shirt, making it billow out behind me, yanking me backward so I had to stop climbing and wrap my elbows around the scaffolding. I was also pretty sure I could feel the entire structure swaying.

The lightning got more and more frequent, too, and the thunder was almost constant by the time I got up to where my father and uncle were. They were both crouched down on a flat expanse of wooden boards, next to a huge array of lights that was tied down under a sheet of plastic. Michael reached out, took my hand, and pulled me up next to him.

Once I had stopped climbing, I could tell for certain that the tower was swaying from side to side in the high winds. At this height, the movement had to be a couple of feet in each direction. "Please come down now, Davey!" Michael yelled. "Somebody's going to get hurt up here."

A boom of thunder came then, so intense that I could feel it shaking the tower even amid all of the other noise and motion that was going on. Michael reached out to David with one hand and to me with the other, yanking us downward until all three of us were lying on the wooden platform with our heads together in the middle.

"You shouldn't have followed me, Michael," David said. "Besides, what do you care, anyway? You said you just want to get away from me for a while."

"That's not what I said, David. I asked you how you would feel if I had to go away for a while. I didn't say I wanted to."

"Yeah, who would want to go live with Willow when they could stay with me and Mom and Dad in hell?"

"David, that's not what's happening. I swear I'm not moving in with Willow."

"Then what is going on, man? You're going to get your own apartment, so you can just party with your chick whenever you want to? It's still the same thing for me. I should have known when you suddenly changed your mind and got me the ticket for this festival that you felt guilty about something. And now I know what. Looks like this was my bye-bye weekend, huh?"

This was like watching a slow-motion train wreck. I could see and hear every little excruciating detail, and I was totally terrified, but I didn't have the power to save anybody.

"It's not like that, Davey."

"Then what is it like? Tell me, Michael. That way, when you're gone and there's nobody to help me when Mom and Dad are bossing me around and passing out all weekend, at least I'll know why."

It was almost completely nighttime dark tucked in there between the huge lights and the wood sheeting, except when the lightning flashed. Just then, the sky lit up and I could actually feel the hair on my arms stand at attention. I wasn't sure which was scarier: the thought of getting fried by a zillion volts and then thrown from the sky, or the pain of watching my father say things to his brother that he would never have time to take back.

In the sudden flat-white glare, Michael looked like he was already a ghost. "I can't, Davey. I can't tell you. Please believe me. It's for your own good. Can't you trust me?"

David rose to his knees. Michael did, too.

David looked like he was about to smash something. Michael just looked sick. I rose up as well, and inched my way backward so I was near the edge of the platform. I was more scared than ever, but I had a feeling that was the right place to be.

"Yeah, I can trust you. I can trust you to leave me. I can trust you to ditch me, then tell me it's for my own good, like I'm still some stupid little five-year-old. I can trust you to dose my brownies so you can go off into the woods and ball with your girlfriend, then lie to me about it. I can—"

Over the storm, I didn't hear the smack, but I saw my father's head rock backward, and I braced myself to catch him if he tumbled into me. In the next lightning flash, I saw that Michael had grabbed the front of David's shirt with his other hand before slapping him across the face.

Even in that moment of awful fury, Michael had thought of his little brother's safety.

Michael lowered David down slowly until he was lying, curled in a ball, on the wood. Then he turned to me and said, "I've never hit him before. I just—I don't know what to do anymore." It's pretty hard to tell whether someone is crying in the middle of a massive thunderstorm, but there wasn't any doubt in my mind that my uncle was. He took off his own shirt, balled it up, and tried to push it against David's nose, which had started to bleed in great spattering gushes. David pushed his brother's hand away.

I took the shirt in my own hands as Michael began to mutter over and over, "I'm sorry, Davey. I'm so sorry." I wrung the water out of the fabric as best I could, and then held it out to David, who took it and pressed it against his face.

We sat there for a while, nobody making eye contact with anybody else, as the tower rocked and swayed. Then I noticed that my father was shivering so violently I could see his shoulder bouncing off the platform. "David," I said, putting my hand on his shoulder, "are you all right?"

"C-cold," he grunted through clenched teeth. His whole body was bucking, and his teeth were chattering.

"Michael, we have to get David down from here now," I said. "I think he might be going into shock."

Michael nodded and took one of David's hands. I grabbed David's belt from the other side, and we gradually coaxed him backward to the edge of the wooden platform. At that point, the rain was so heavy that I didn't think David could hear me, but I urged him along the way you'd keep a horse or a little kid moving. I was going, "Come on, buddy! You can do it, pal!" every couple of inches.

Michael's eyes met mine as he slid his own legs over the side onto the rungs of the tower, and he mouthed, "One . . . two . . . THREE!" I twisted myself around so that my legs were dangling for a moment, until my feet found that first rung, and then I tugged at David's waist until his body swung around and over.

The first step was the most horrifying, because for a second or two, Michael and I each had to let go of the platform with one arm and lean back to allow David's body to swing into the space between us. It felt for a second like I was going to tumble backward, but then David's feet hit the first metal ledge. I threw my weight forward again and just leaned there for a moment, my weight half on my father's waist and half on the platform.

I couldn't stay still for long, though. First of all, as soon as I stopped moving, I could feel my father's body shaking all over again. Second of all, a huge flash of lightning startled me so much I almost flinched—and in our situation, flinching was an extremely bad idea. Michael reached his arm across David's back and tapped my wrist. I nodded. We locked arms around David's waist and started the long climb down.

I have never been so frightened in my entire life. David was in bad shape, and his feet kept slipping. Between the stitched-up cuts, the rain, his drugged-up state, and the constant tremors, it was going to take a near-miracle for him to get down without falling off.

And if David died, I would never be born.

After about ten feet, he stopped moving his legs completely and just clung on to one of the metal beams with both arms.

A bolt of lightning came so close that I actually felt a *zing!* run through me. "Come on!" I yelled, an inch from David's ear. I'm sure Michael was shouting in his other ear, too, but I couldn't hear it. David leaned his forehead against the tower, closed his eyes, and started saying, "No! No! No!" over and over. I couldn't exactly hear him, but I'd known my dad long enough to lip-read that particular word.

Now he sounded like the father I had grown up with. I started shouting at the top of my lungs, "YES! YES! YES!"

He never stopped saying no, and it made me madder and madder for some crazy reason. After all the times he wouldn't let me do things my whole life—after all the times he wouldn't pay attention to me, or tell me anything about his past, or let me see my friends, or even hug me—was I really going to actually and literally get KILLED because my father finally said no to me one time too many?

I flipped out. Right in the middle of the storm, however many feet up, with death flashing and flaring all around me, I dug my hand into my dad's shoulder and unloaded:

"Move it! Who the hell do you think you are? You want to get yourself fried up here? You want Michael to die? You want me to die? And what about your wife? What about your kid? You fucking quitter! You coward! You loser! Boo hoo! 'My brother said he might leave me! I'm just going to curl up and die now!' Well, I don't give a shit! You can't give up your whole damn life because of what happens to someone else. Now move! Just move! I said MOVE YOUR FUCKING FEET!"

David looked at me, then down, then at Michael, then back at me. Finally, he took a step downward.

In the end, I was the one who slipped.

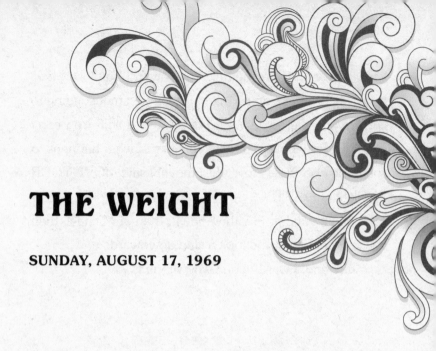

THE WEIGHT

SUNDAY, AUGUST 17, 1969

Woodstock saved me. I guess somebody must have looked up and seen us struggling to get down from the tower, and that somebody must have poked somebody else. Somehow, those first two somebodies turned into a human pyramid that reached high enough to grab me when I fell. They got my father and my uncle, too.

Think about that. You won't see it in the official movie. There's no way cameras would have worked through all that rain and lightning anyway. But how many people must it have taken to get us down safely? Twenty-five? Fifty? And they all got together without any orders, or badges, or bullhorns, in the face of real danger. Plenty of people I know would have just burrowed down in the mud and waited it out. Nobody could have blamed them if they had, right?

But instead, this crowd of random teenagers locked arms, stood shoulder to shoulder, leaned against the cold metal, prayed away the lightning, and piled on, level after level. I figure it probably took three layers to reach high enough.

Then somebody got to us. Fifteen feet up? Twenty? And just when my bones and muscles had had it, when I couldn't shout any longer, when my whole self skipped a beat—the spirit of the festival itself reached out through outstretched arms and lifted us up and away.

I was handed down from person to person. It occurs to me now that maybe David, Michael, and I were the first crowd-surfers. Who knows? At the time, my heart was beating so hard, and the rain was pounding into my up-turned face so viciously, that all I could think about was not gagging. But before I knew it, the three of us were being carried to one of the medical tents.

With my amazing luck, it was the same tent we had visited the night before. At first, the three of us were placed on three adjacent cots, but Michael popped up to explain that he wasn't injured or anything. I sat on the edge of my cot, but felt kind of dizzy, so I didn't stand right away. I looked around and saw that we were almost the only three patients, aside from one guy a few cots away, who appeared to be sleeping with his back to us. The same nurse was there, and she recognized David and me instantly. She shooed away the kids who had carried us in before we could even thank them, and then asked David, "What happened this time?"

David was shivering too hard to talk, so the nurse immediately pulled his shirt off and started drying him with a towel. Then she wrapped him up in a brownish army blanket and asked me, "Listen, Betty Crocker, what did your friend take now?"

"Umm . . ." I said.

"The same brownies?"

I nodded. It sounded pretty stupid when she said it out loud like that.

"You have got to be freaking kidding me! All right, is he physically injured?"

Michael said, "Uh, he got hit in the nose. And I think he's really cold."

She turned to me and said, "Who's the detective?"

"This is his older brother, Michael."

"Well, older brother Michael, let's have a look. I'm warning you, I'm about five seconds away from getting your brother choppered out of here. In fact, I should have done that last night when I stitched him up, but—"

"Stitched him up?" Michael barked. Apparently, he hadn't been listening so well when David had come back to the blanket and told him about our adventure the previous night.

"Umm, long story?" I said.

"Anyway, nothing's flying right now, so it's irrelevant. Let me take a quick look at your brother. His name's David, right? If he looks physically okay, and he's responsive, he can sleep this off here. If he's physically okay, but freaking out, then I'll have to send him over to the bad trips tent. If there's a real medical issue going on here, then we'll have to call your parents and start looking into either an ambulance or a helicopter for when the weather clears."

She leaned over David with a bag of instruments and started examining him. I leaned back and rubbed my eyes. She couldn't call David's parents. That would ruin everything. Even though we were rapidly running out of time to meet Jimi Hendrix, it still could happen. I knew the weather had to clear, and the rest of the bands had to play. Then the announcer might call us up to the stage. Jimi could meet us.

And then . . . what? What could possibly happen in less than a day that would change the entire history of my family?

The nurse stood up after a few minutes and said, "The good news is that, aside from a black eye, I think David's body is going to be as good as new once he's had a chance to get warmed up for a while. The bad news is that he won't talk to me. In fact, he won't look at me.

"When a patient who's taken a hallucinogenic drug is unresponsive like this, my instructions are to go down to the big med tent and get a doctor."

"Wait," I said. "What's the doctor going to do?"

"Son, if the doctor can't get your friend to respond, we're going to have to shoot him up with Thorazine and fly him out to the hospital. This doesn't usually happen from mushrooms, but once in a while, a kid uses one of these drugs and just doesn't come back. Now wait here, all right? The big tent is a little ways from here, and the docs are pretty busy, but I'll be back as soon as I can. Until then, keep David warm, and whatever you do—don't let him go anywhere."

The nurse jogged out into the storm, and Michael ran a hand through his hair. "What are we going to do?" he said. "They can't call our parents, man. Dad will kill David. He'll kill me, too, but he's crazy about drugs. He'll just kill David. We have to wake David up. Goddamn, it wasn't supposed to be like this. I just wanted my little brother to come hear some groovy music, and now—"

"Music! That's it!" I said. "Michael, you have to go get your guitar!"

"What?"

"John Sebastian told me last night. He spent the whole

day playing his guitar for people in the bad trips tent, and the music mellowed them out. If we do that for David, he won't need the drugs or the helicopter or anything, right? But we have to do it before the doctor gets here!"

Michael stared at me for a second, then bolted out of the tent. I sat there alone with my father and the sleeping guy, both of whom were turned away from me. Aside from the occasional whistling gust of wind, the storm seemed to be getting quieter, which was probably a bad thing. Now all it meant was that they'd be able to chopper David out sooner.

"David?" I called quietly. My father didn't even twitch. "David, can you hear me?" Nothing. I tiptoed over and peeked at his face. His eyes were closed, but not in the relaxed way that people's eyes close for sleep. David's eyelids were clenched shut. I didn't know if he was awake and lost in a terrifying trip, or if he was too angry to deal with the world, or what—but I knew things were going disastrously wrong. I felt like I was watching the friendly, bouncing David of Friday morning enter a cocoon, and I knew if I let this happen, he would emerge as the closed-up dad I had always known.

"Come on, David," I said. "You have to wake up. I need you." *That won't make any sense to him,* I thought. *Why would some kid he met two days ago need him? On the other hand, you just had a screaming breakdown at him on the tower, and he's not responding anyway, so what's the point of holding back now?*

I could feel myself hyperventilating. It almost felt like the air was being sucked out of the tent. "You have to come back. I need you. Your brother needs you. I know you don't think he does, but he's in danger. And you need to wake up, or you're going to get sent home from the festival right now. And if you get sent home from the festival, everything's going to get all messed up. The whole future's going to change. I might not even be *born*! And I won't meet Jimi Hendrix. And we won't get his guitar. So I won't save Michael. And I won't *ever* get back to my own time, and—"

The flap door of the tent burst open. David didn't respond to the sound, but I jumped straight up in the air. It was Michael, with the guitar. He was gasping so hard that he handed the case to me and said, "Play. I . . . can't . . . breathe." Then he collapsed onto the edge of David's cot.

I picked up the towel the nurse had used on David, and dried off Michael's guitar case as quickly as I could. Then Michael said, "Forget the case—no time!"

Wow, I thought. *His brother truly is worth more to him than his Martin.*

I took the guitar out, and strummed a few chords. Amazingly, it was in tune despite the humidity, so I started playing songs right away. I sang the most soothing old

206

songs I could think of. David didn't miraculously sit up and recover or anything, so I kept on playing song after song.

Then I thought of the saddest and most beautiful song I know, Jimi Hendrix's "Angel." It's also incredibly tough to play, but I thought maybe it would bring some kind of strange good luck. I mean, it's all about an angel coming down from heaven to rescue the singer. Which was kind of what I was trying to be, but also what we all needed.

I played and sang my heart out. At the end, my throat was raw, and my fingers ached from the stretches it took to reach all the notes. Jimi Hendrix had huge hands; I don't. When I stopped, David rolled halfway over, so he was looking straight up at the ceiling. He didn't say anything, though. Michael did. "Wow, what was that? It's beautiful, man. Haunting."

"Oh, it's a song called 'Angel.' It's on a Jimi Hendrix album called—"

A quiet, shaky voice rose up from the cot in the corner. "That song's never been on any album. And, well, I think I would know if it had."

The form on the cot threw off its blanket, sat up, and spoke. "Please allow me to introduce myself. My name is James. But, you know, my friends call me Jimi."

MESSAGE TO LOVE

SUNDAY, AUGUST 17, 1969

I nearly dropped Michael's guitar. "Uh ... uh ..." I said.

Michael was a little smoother. He managed to say actual words. "Hendrix. You're Jimi Hendrix!"

Jimi, who was wearing a fringed white leather jacket, and sporting an earring and a fluorescent pink bandana over his Afro, looked rather sheepish about our shock. "Yes, I am," he said softly.

"But ... but ... you were sleeping!" I exclaimed. Because, you know, rock stars don't just sleep. Or because I'm an idiot.

Jimi said, "Well, man, I was tired, you know. It's crazy backstage, and everybody wants something from you all the time. And, well, I may have swallowed some, you know, *recreational pharmaceuticals*, so things were feeling a little tripped out. So I just kind of wandered in here and asked the nurse if I could crash for a while. Where is she?"

"She went looking for a doctor and some Thorazine," Michael said. "My brother, David, here ate some mushrooms, and now he's having a bad trip. He won't even open his eyes. She said if David doesn't wake up, the doctor's going to shoot him up with it, call our parents, and send him to the hospital. And our parents are going to kill us. Our father isn't . . . Well, he's not the kind of father you'd want to have. I mean, if you had a choice."

"Wow, that's too bad, man. I know all about that scene."

"You do?" Michael asked. "But—"

"But what?" Jimi asked, again in that gentle voice.

"But you're a rock star. You're a hero of mine. You're, um, I mean, this sounds stupid, but you're the whole reason I wanted to come to this concert. Why would you have a bad trip? Everything in your life is a dream, right?"

Jimi smiled, but he didn't look happy. "Just because my life is your dream doesn't mean it's mine. What's your name?"

"I'm Michael and this is Gabriel."

"Michael, don't mind me, all right? I'm just really tired, and too many people want me to be too many things, you know? Everybody *wants* something. Sometimes I wish I could just curl up and hide away for a year or so. But I can't.

"And your dad . . . I know all about fathers. Trust me. So, Gabriel?"

"Uh, yes. Sir. Yes, sir."

Jimi laughed. "I left the army a couple of years ago, Gabriel. I don't think anybody calls lead guitar players 'sir.' You know what I'm saying?"

I nodded and gulped.

"Anyway," he said, "how did you know my song? It has *not* been on an album. Plus, you changed the lyrics around. I've recorded a couple of demos, and the lines are a little bit different from how you sang them. Tell me again where you heard it?"

Oh, boy. I had really screwed up. This was probably the most awkward moment of my life. No, the most awkward moment of anyone's life. Now that I had a moment to think, I was pretty sure the "Angel" song was on an album of previously unreleased material that had come out after Jimi Hendrix died.

Try explaining that one. "I, well, uh . . . Michael, can I speak to Jimi alone for a minute?"

Michael looked at me like I was crazy. So did Jimi. And maybe I was crazy. But somehow, thinking about the note Jimi was going to write me, I felt like I could tell him more of the truth than I could tell my uncle. After a long pause, Michael said, "Okay, I'll just sit by my brother here."

Jimi gestured me over to his cot. I handed the guitar to

Michael and walked over. Jimi said, "All right, little brother. Tell me about the song."

I tried to say something, but no sound came from my throat.

"Please?" he whispered, licking his lips. "It's important to me."

"Why?" I asked.

"Because I *know* where you came from," he said.

I felt sick. Who knew how badly this was going to mess everything up? "What do you mean?" I said.

"I heard you, Gabriel. When you were talking to David. I heard the whole thing. You talked about the future. And how you might not get to be born. And how you needed to get back to your own time. Then when you played 'Angel,' I knew—you're a time traveler! I've been waiting for you to come, you know."

"What?"

"That's right, brother—I've been waiting. Have you ever listened to my song lyrics?"

"Sure. I'm a huge fan. But—"

"But nothing. Why do you think I'm always singing about flying saucers and aliens and angels? And mermaids? And traveling through time? You were the only one I was still waiting on, man!"

"You mean . . . ?"

He grinned. "Everybody else already showed up, man."

My mouth dropped open. He had to be joking. But then again, I was a kid from the future, so why couldn't there be flying saucers and aliens? Aliens? Angels? "Really? Seriously?"

He nodded, an extremely serious look on his face. "Mermaids?" I asked.

Jimi raised an eyebrow and giggled. "All right, I'm kidding you," he said. "No, I'm not. Yes, I am. No, I'm not. Yes, I am."

"Wait, which is it?"

"Really," he said, "if you want to know God's honest truth, I'm a little bit high." He giggled one more time, and it dawned on me that Jimi Hendrix—an incredibly famous rock star—sounded nervous. "And, well, an old fortune-teller lady over in Europe gave me a guitar, and told me I was going to meet a boy from the future. So, Gabriel, are you the one?"

I inhaled deeply, then nodded. "Yes."

"Wow," he said. "I always thought you'd have some kind of, I don't know, silver clothes or something. Your hair is pretty cool, though. Does everybody have hair like that where you're from?"

"No, my hair was black until two days ago. Then I played your white guitar, and, well, it zapped me back here. Somehow, the time change bleached my hair."

"You played my white guitar, huh? Well, that makes

sense. The gypsy lady laid a whole big trip on me. She said I would play a song this year that would change everything for my country, and the guitar I played it on would become—what did she say?—the symbol and center of these three days. That guitar was the one she gave to me."

I nodded. I knew exactly what song she meant. After all, it was the most famous scene in the Woodstock movie.

"So, I just got my new band together for this festival, Gabriel, and we're still not really tight, you know? What song am I supposed to play that's so important? I hope it's not 'Angel,' because these boys don't even know that one!"

I licked my lips. Holy cow, I could completely change the future by not mentioning "The Star-Spangled Banner." When Jimi Hendrix had played that song early on Monday morning as Woodstock drew to a close, he reclaimed America and its anthem for a new generation. It was huge. I mean, I wasn't sure I fully understood it, but my mom had once said that that moment showed the world for once and for all that you could be patriotic and still hate the Vietnam War. She even thought it had helped make the war end sooner.

" 'The Star-Spangled Banner'."

"Oh, really? I've played that one before, and it hasn't been some huge deal or anything."

"Well, tomorrow it will be."

"Tomorrow? I'm playing tonight."

"Nope."

"You're kidding me now."

"Nope." Hey, this was kind of fun.

"Because of the rain?"

"Yup."

"Wow, far out. So, I just, like, *give* you my white Strat, huh? And how does it become a, you know, time machine? Does everyone in the distant future have a special time cube in their flying saucer that lets them triangulate back from an object to its source, or whatever you want to call it?"

No, I thought, *but that would be really freaking cool.* "I don't know about the distant future. My time is only forty-five years from now. That kid lying on the cot over there? The one that's not moving or anything? He's going to be my dad. Michael's my uncle. I, uh, I came back to save Michael."

"Wait a minute," Jimi said. "You have to tell me about the guitar."

"Okay, you have to give it to Michael after you come offstage tomorrow morning, with a note that tells me what to do. And what I have to do is play your chord."

"My chord?"

"You know, the E seventh chord with the sharp ninth in it, like in 'Purple Haze'? Or 'Foxy Lady'? You're going to give Michael the guitar, with a note that tells me to play the chord for a three-day pass."

"What happens at the end of three days?"

"I don't know yet."

"Wait a minute, you're saying that fifty years in the future, people are still going to know my songs?"

I thought about this. Jimi was going to die at age twenty-seven in 1970, but obviously he didn't know this. So in fifty years, he'd only be twenty-six plus fifty, or seventy-six. That wasn't even so old. "Sure," I said. "You'll be playing concerts and stuff, and you'll be on TV all the time. It'll be really—"

"Gabriel, I know I'm going to die soon," Jimi said. "You don't have to lie to me about it. The gypsy lady told me, but I've always known anyway. My mother died young, and she was the only person who ever really cared about me. That's what the song 'Angel' is about, right? It's about joining my mother again in the sky someday. So you don't have to pretend for me. I've been waiting for you to come so I can find out whether my life has made a difference. I want to know people won't just forget me right away, man."

"Forget you? Are you kidding me? You're huge in fifty years. You know how you said, 'When the power of love overcomes the love of power, the world will know peace?'"

"Yeah, so?"

"That was, like, everybody's favorite Facebook status in seventh grade."

"Everybody's favorite *what*?"

"It's, uh . . . it means that . . . well, everybody is going to

215

have little computers in their phones, okay? And they're going to carry the phones around. And when seventh-grade girls are trying to sound smart and deep, they're all going to type your quote into their little computer-phone things for everyone else to see."

"Far out."

"Yeah. And your music. Guitar players are going to study you in school the way classical players study Mozart and Bach. Please trust me: You don't have to worry about your legacy."

"They're going to study me? Really? I don't even know how to read music, man."

"You know how to play it, though."

Jimi looked down at his feet. "Can I ask you something else?"

"Sure. We have to hurry, though. My father—"

"I know. I really need to know this, though. When I die . . . Do you know . . . Will my family come?"

"What do you mean?"

"I mean . . . listen, this hasn't been in any magazine articles or anything, but my father didn't let me or my brother, Leon, go to our mother's funeral. I've had nightmares about it ever since. Nightmares about my mother trying to reach me and ask me why I didn't come to her, and nightmares about my father and Leon not coming to stand by me."

Jimi swallowed before continuing. "So, uh, do they? When it's my time, do they come and stand for me?"

Oh, man. I knew the answer to this one. "Mr. Hendrix—Jimi—when the time comes, your father and your brother will be there. They won't leave you. I read a book about your life, and I know this. Your father will stand over your casket, and at the funeral, in front of everybody, he's going to reach down and rub his knuckles over your head again and again. He's going to say, 'My boy, my boy, my boy,' until someone leads him away and they close the coffin. Your father won't leave your side until you're in the ground. And then he's going to spend the rest of his life running a museum dedicated to you."

Tears ran down Jimi's face. "Thank you," he whispered. "Ever since I was a little kid, I've been so worried I'd be alone when my time comes. But for the first time now, I'm not afraid. It won't be so bad, going, if I know my father will be there for me. That's true, right?"

I nodded.

"You promise?"

I nodded again.

Jimi Hendrix leaned back and smiled. I looked over at my own father, who still hadn't moved an inch. Michael was rubbing his shoulders and whispering to him, but it didn't appear to be working. I felt a lump in my throat. Jimi Hendrix had been abused and neglected by his father his entire life, and his greatest relief was that once he was dead, his dad would mourn him. My dad was alive and breathing across the room, and I was alive and breathing right here.

Maybe, if things went right, I wouldn't have to settle for cold comfort.

"Thank you," Jimi said.

"No problem. But, listen. If you stop taking so many pills . . . or if you don't drink any red wine . . . maybe you could—"

Jimi turned so we were facing each other head on. "Gabriel," he said, "my future is already done. You read about it, right?"

I nodded a third time.

"But yours isn't," he continued. "You came back here for a reason, right? I've been waiting so long for your message to me that I forgot you must be on your own mission. You said you have to save your uncle?"

I nodded yet again. But my heart was suddenly pounding. Because Jimi had just said, "My future is already done. You already read about it, right?" If that was how things worked, Uncle Mike's future was already done, too. If Jimi Hendrix was right, I wasn't at Woodstock to save anybody's life.

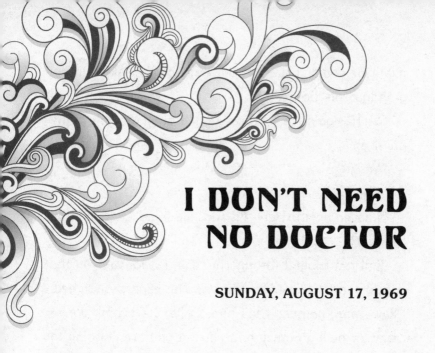

I DON'T NEED
NO DOCTOR

SUNDAY, AUGUST 17, 1969

"**H**eroin, huh?" Jimi asked, very quietly.

"Yes."

"Eight weeks?"

"From Friday. I'm pretty sure he used it for the first time last night. He has this plan to get out of going to Vietnam. He's supposed to report for his physical in October, so he's going to shoot up a bunch of times between now and then. He thinks the army doctors will see the track marks in his arm, and he'll be all high and messed up, so they'll reject him, and he won't have to go."

"Man, doesn't he know people die behind that stuff?"

"Yeah, but he's desperate." Lowering my voice even more, I laid out the whole scenario about my grandfather, the stuff my uncle had heard him say, and the reasons why my uncle couldn't stand to leave my brother alone in my grandparents' house.

"So he's going to overdose right around the time of the physical?"

"Yes."

"But you haven't told him yet?"

"I haven't come right out and said it, no. Do you think I should?"

Jimi ran a hand through his hair, sat forward on the edge of the cot, leaned his elbows on his knees, and sighed. "Naw, man, you can't tell him. Either he'll think you're crazy, or he'll go crazy himself. But you aren't going to save his life. It's like with me, Gabriel: As far as you're concerned, your uncle is already dead."

"But—"

"Listen to me, now. I wish all the time that old lady hadn't told me I was going to die. I can't stop it. I can't change anything. All she did was make sure I never had another night of peaceful dreams for whatever nights I have left. I'm twenty-six years old, Gabriel, and I already feel ancient inside. Whatever dreams your uncle has left—at least let some of them be good ones, all right?"

What do you say when a doomed genius of rock lays all that on you? I never had to figure out a reply, because just then, my father groaned. Michael said, "Gabriel, come here!" I jumped up, and so did Jimi Hendrix.

"David, can you hear me?" Michael asked.

David, who had been curled up in a tight ball, rolled onto his back and replied, "If I say yes, are you going to hit me again?"

"Oh, Davey, I'm so sorry," my uncle said, dropping to his knees next to the cot and throwing his arms around my father's head and shoulders.

After a moment, David freed his arms from the blankets and hugged his brother back. Then he said, "Please don't leave me with Mom and Dad. Please."

I couldn't see Michael's face, but his voice sounded like he was all choked up as he answered, "I'm trying, David."

Jimi and I stood around awkwardly for a few minutes while the two brothers made up. Eventually, David looked past Michael and noticed that there was a full-fledged rock god standing over his cot. "Holy cow!" he shouted. "You're—"

"Don't say it, man," Jimi said, laughing. "You'll make me blush. But yeah, I am. How're you feeling? Your friend Gabriel was pretty freaked out about you."

"I'm all right. But wait, how did I get here? All I remember is being up on that platform thing. And it was pouring. And there was thunder. And I was really cold. And then Michael hit me—"

"I said I was sorry."

"I know, I'm just saying what happened. Anyway, then

we were climbing down the tower, and I didn't want to go any farther. So then someone started shouting in my ear."

My heart skipped. *Oh, geez,* I thought. *What if he remembers all the crazy stuff I was yelling at him?* "Listen, David, I didn't know what I was saying up there. I was just shouting any nutty thing that came into my head to get you to, uh, you know—"

David cut me off. "It wasn't you. I remember now. It was Michael. But what he was saying didn't make any sense." He turned and stared right into his brother's eyes as though Jimi and I weren't even there. "We need to talk later. Do you promise?"

Michael said, "I promise."

The flap of the tent flew open, and a gust of wind blasted in. "Hey, it's a party!" a female voice exclaimed. "And this time I brought the drugs!"

The nurse shouldered her way past me, holding an alarmingly large syringe. "Wait," Michael said, "my brother doesn't need the shot. He's awake now, see? He's not even confused or anything. Right, David?"

David was staring at the needle like it was a king cobra swaying over him. "Yeah, I'm fine! I swear. I was just, um, really tired before. But now that I've had a little nap, I'm all better. So I can just grab my clothes and be on my way if that's okay with—"

"Not so fast, buddy! I have children your age, and I wouldn't want them running around in some godforsaken muddy field, all stitched up, dosing themselves with Lord knows what—TWICE—and then getting sent out to do it all over again a third time. What would your mother say if she were here?"

"Well, what time is it?"

The nurse looked at her highly efficient-looking watch. "Around five thirty. Why?"

"Because on weekends, my mother is pretty drunk by five thirty. So she probably wouldn't say much."

The nurse didn't know how to respond to this, so we all just stood around for a moment as the syringe wavered in the air. It seemed obvious to me that she wasn't going to give David the shot if he wasn't catatonic or raving insanely, but the likelihood of her shipping him out on a helicopter still seemed pretty darn high.

Then Jimi swung into action. He flashed a brilliant, toothy grin and said, "Ma'am, you said you have children as old as David? Really?"

"Yes, I do. Why?"

"Well, I just found it hard to believe that such a young-looking lady could possibly be the mother of teenagers, that's all."

This had to be the oldest line in the book, even back in 1969, but the nurse actually batted her eyes and blushed.

"Oh, come on, now. Quit teasing an old lady and let me figure out what to do with your friend here."

"All right, I'll tell you what. Do you happen to know who I am, by any chance?"

"What do you mean? All I know is that you're a young man who needed a place to rest for a while. A flirtatious young man."

Jimi laughed. "That's all true. But I'm also a musician. In fact, I'm scheduled to play at this concert later on tonight. If you'd like, I'd be glad to sign autographs for your kids if you'll just let my friend come with me now. I'll take him to one of the management trailers backstage, and he can rest in bed there. We have security and everything, so I can assure you he'll be quite comfortable."

The nurse said, "You're one of the performers? What's your name?"

David said, "He's Jimi Hendrix! He's huge! I have a poster of him in my room! He's the whole reason I wanted to come here in the first place. And now he's right here next to me—can you believe it?"

The nurse said, "Is this boy telling the truth? Are you really Jimi Hendrix?"

Jimi nodded.

The nurse said, "I have a son and a daughter, and they both LOVE your music. They're not going to believe this! Can I get your autograph for them?"

"Anything for you, sweetheart," Jimi said.

"Oh, my kids are going to think their mother is so far out!" the nurse said. Then she giggled. She actually giggled. "But David, you are still going to have to prove to me that you're all right. Jimi—may I call you Jimi?"

"As long as you call me."

"Oh, stop!"

"Jimi, take your friend Gabriel over to the other side of the tent so I can ask David some questions and do a few little medical tests, all right? If everything checks out, I'll release him to your care. . . . God help us all. After you sign some autographs for my kids."

Five minutes later, we were standing at the flap of the tent, about to push our way back out into the early evening. Our nurse pointed the syringe right in our faces and growled, "I had better not see you back here again. Got that?"

Michael, David, and I nodded.

Then she smiled, and her voice got kind of throaty. "Except you, Jimi. You're welcome to pop in if you, well, need anything."

"I'll keep that in mind, ma'am," Jimi said. You always hear about all the terrible stuff rock stars do, but I have to say, in my experience, several of them are extremely polite.

We stepped out of the tent, and I expected to be

spattered with rain, but to my surprise, I could actually see the last rays of the setting sun peeking through the clouds. "Well, what now?" I asked.

We all turned to Jimi. "I kind of have to get backstage, you know? My manager probably thinks I split by now. It's going to be some kind of huge hassle if I don't make the scene."

Without another word, he turned and started to walk away.

Michael, David, and I just stood there, crestfallen. I know this sounds lame, but when you're hanging out with a star, and he's been talking about taking you behind the scenes, everything feels kind of electric. You feel more than alive. And then, when he suddenly just walks away, you can't help feeling empty.

When Jimi was fifteen feet away or so, he turned around so fast that the fringes on his jacket whirled away from his body. Then he gave us that smile. "Hey, what's the matter, gentlemen? Are you coming or not?"

My first thought, in the excitement of the moment, was YEAH! Then Michael said, "We'd love to. But we have some girls waiting for us back at our blankets, so . . ."

Jimi laughed. Then he said, "Michael, man, there's always room for a few extra chicks backstage. Let's go get 'em."

David said, "You mean, you're going to walk with us?"

Jimi said, "Sure, why not? I have legs and everything, don't I?"

"But won't the crowd, like, go crazy or something?"

"Not if you be cool, man. It's getting dark, right? So people aren't going to go all crazy about me unless we give them a reason to start staring. Now, here's what's going to happen. Michael is going to walk first. I'm going to follow. You and Gabriel are going to walk behind me like it's no big deal, all right? As long as we all act normal, so will everybody else. That's how life works. Now watch and learn. Michael?"

Michael started walking.

AMAZING JOURNEY

SUNDAY, AUGUST 17, 1969

Jimi was right: Nobody looked twice at him. In fact, when we found the girls, they didn't even notice we had brought somebody back with us; they immediately started yelling at Michael and me. Willow was the loudest. She was all like, "Mike, what in the world is going on? You come back here, grab your guitar, and go charging off into the storm again without a word of explanation. We were worried sick about you! If you think I'm going to just sit around like a trained pet while you run around having adventures, you've got another think coming! I ought to—"

This went on for a while, with a stereo contribution from Debbie, and didn't stop until Tina burst out with,

"Hey, David, who's your friend? Holy shit, he looks just like Jimi Hendrix!"

Two minutes later, we were packing up our damp, muddy stuff. Fifteen minutes later, we were all holding official-looking passes, and we were standing BACK-STAGE AT WOODSTOCK. My mind kept seeing it that way, in capital letters. Every few minutes, I would think, *Hey, are you having fun BACKSTAGE AT WOODSTOCK?* Or, *Boy, the sodas sure do taste better BACKSTAGE AT WOODSTOCK!* Jimi told us that the stage had been built on a gigantic turntable so that bands could be revolved on and off quickly, but by Sunday night, the mechanism was broken, and band and crew members and their friends were standing everywhere behind the amplifiers and PA system watching each group perform. While David and I explained the past few hours' events to Tina and Debbie, and Michael whispered intensely with Willow, we watched Country Joe perform for his second time at the festival, this time with his band, the Fish. Meanwhile, Jimi was snatched away by his managers, just as he'd said he would be.

A while later, I was making out with Debbie BACK-STAGE AT WOODSTOCK when Jimi tapped me on the shoulder. "Can I talk to you for a minute?" he asked. I said yes, because really, when Jimi Hendrix asks you for a moment of your time BACKSTAGE AT WOODSTOCK, that's what you do. He grabbed Michael, too, and told David to keep an eye on all three girls at all times. "I'm serious, man," Jimi said. "You can trust me, but some of these other rock-and-roll cats are pigs when it comes to women. Seriously."

And with that comforting mixed metaphor, he whisked me away with my uncle, over the rickety wooden footbridge and into a trailer. "Sorry to take you away from the music, but I had to ask you a couple of things. First, a question for Gabriel. I'm supposed to be the last act of the whole festival. But now things are running so late because of the rain that they want me to go on at midnight tonight. But then I wouldn't be last anymore—you dig? And I want to close out the festival.

"What do you think? The organizers are saying if I go on at midnight, the audience will be bigger, but I still think I should hold out, and let the all the other bands play before me."

Michael asked, "Why are you asking a kid? Shouldn't you ask your manager or something?"

Of course, I knew why Jimi was asking me—he was just verifying what I had already told him would happen. And I knew Michael was just asking in order to find out what Jimi knew.

"Mike," I said, "Jimi and I had a long talk before, okay? He needed some advice from me, that's all. Jimi, you're going to close out the concert."

Jimi turned to Michael. "Now, we have some unfinished business from back at the medical tent."

"We do?"

"Yeah. Gabriel tells me you've got yourself in a bit of a situation with Uncle Sam. I've been there myself, man. I don't know if you know this, but I was in the hundred and first airborne division back in '62. Then I broke my ankle, and that was the end of my life as a paratrooper, dig?"

"Wow, I didn't know that."

"I'm not really into talking about it much."

I knew why Jimi didn't like to talk about it, because I had read it in his biography. When the army started holding back his musical career, he had lied to a bunch of army psychologists in order to get discharged early. Nobody seemed to be 100 percent sure exactly what he had said, but the rumor was that he had pretended to be gay, which was a surefire way to horrify the army back in the sixties, but also a surefire way to mess up your reputation in the rock-music world at the time. When he talked about the discharge to reporters, he had always claimed it was because of an ankle injury.

"Anyway, yeah, I got my draft notice a few weeks ago. And I can't do it. I can't go."

"Why not? Army life isn't so terrible, brother. Really."

I wasn't sure how much Michael would reveal to Jimi—who, after all, was a total stranger—but he absolutely unloaded. Jimi and I both just sat and listened as Michael told us stuff that burned a hole in my heart forever.

"You want to know why I could never fight in a war, man? You're probably just going to think it's stupid. I mean, I've never told this to anybody, not even Willow. Davey was there, but he didn't see most of it, and I don't think he would remember it, anyhow. He was too little. I hope to God he doesn't. . . . It's bad enough that I have to.

"I was seven years old. There used to be this little pond on a vacant lot two doors down from our house. It's not there anymore, because they filled it in when they finished the subdivision a few years later. But all the kids in the neighborhood used to play near it, throwing rocks and sticks, building forts, that kind of stuff. You couldn't swim in it or anything, though—it had about a million snapping turtles.

"There were also these beautiful box turtles that would come out and sun themselves on nice days. So one morning, early, I was just sitting there alone. My parents weren't up yet, because they had been partying pretty hard the night before, so I had snuck out to the pond for some peace and quiet before I had to deal with their hangovers and making David's breakfast. I was watching this one turtle sitting on a rock. The turtle wasn't hurting anybody, and neither was I, you know? It was eating a leaf or something, and I was just squatting like a little Indian, checking it out.

"And this huge shadow fell over me. I looked up, and

there was Starkey. He was ten years old, which meant he was at least a head and a half taller than me. He was also a whole hell of a lot meaner, and he had a full-on evil face going at that moment. He asked me, 'Hey, Mikey, wanna guess what today is?'

"I didn't know whether to ignore him or try to humor him. When a big boy was in this kind of mood, it wasn't like either choice was a super-safe bet. I split the difference. I said, 'I don't . . . know?' I remember hating that my voice sounded so weak.

"He shouted, right by my ear, so his spit hit my face, 'It's Turtle Fun Day!'

"I asked him what Turtle Fun Day was, and he reached into the pocket of his pants and pulled out a firecracker. He said, 'You'll like Turtle Fun Day! It's like a science fair and the Fourth of July, all wrapped into one!' Then he reached into his other pocket and whipped out a match-book and a roll of tape. The kid had deep pockets.

"I know the day couldn't actually have stopped being sunny at that exact moment, but when I remember it, it feels that way—like the whole world got cold. I asked him what he meant, and he said, 'Well, Mikey, I have a fun little plan for an experiment, but I only have two hands, so I need an assistant, and you just got picked! Here's what we're gonna do. You grab the turtle and hold it. I'll grab this firecracker and hold it on top of his shell. Then you wrap the tape around the whole turtle and the firecracker a few times so it's stuck on him good and tight. Then I'll light a match and hand it to you so you can start the fuse on the firecracker.'

"I felt sick. I said, 'And then what?'"

"Starkey looked at me like I was a moron. He said, 'What do you mean, and then what? And then BOOM! That's what!'

"I felt even sicker then, like I always felt when I knew my dad was about to belt me. I said, 'No way.'

"Starkey stepped so close to me I could smell him. He had had peanut butter for breakfast. He said, 'You're a pussy, Mikey.'

"What kind of ten-year-old kid calls a seven-year-old a pussy? I've thought about that a lot. But you know what, man? His life had to be a lot like mine. Maybe his parents drank all the time around him and said shit they shouldn't. Maybe they smacked him around, too. I don't know. But I do know I never threatened anybody the way he threatened me that day.

"I said, 'Am not.' I didn't even know what that was, but I could tell it wasn't something I wanted to be.

"He said, 'You're a pussy, Mikey, and you know what else? I stole this firecracker from my big brother, so I have to use it. If I bring it home, I'll have to hide it somewhere and I'll probably get caught with it. That means I've got to use it right now, today. So here's my backup plan. If I can't blow up this turtle, how about I just shove this fire-cracker up your ass and light it?'

"He was bluffing. He had to be. So I decided to call him on it. I said, 'Okay, fine. Why don't you just blow up my . . . butt? If you can catch me!'

"I was just about to run, when I heard David's little four-year-old voice shouting from our backyard, 'Mikey, I'm hungry!'

"The gate between our backyard and the vacant lots was stuck open by rust, and Dad never got around to fix-ing anything, so there was really nothing between David and us but a big empty field. I yelled, 'Stay where you are, Davey!' Now I was scared. First of all, if the shouting woke up our parents, we were both doomed, and second, I didn't want my brother anywhere near Starkey and his fire-crackers. Starkey knew it, too.

"He said, 'Or maybe I could get your little brother to come over here and play? What do you say, Mikey?' Then he started to yell, 'Hey, David—'

"I cut him off. I screamed, 'Go back inside, Davey! I'll come in a minute and make you some toast, all right?'

"I held my breath for a few moments, until I heard our rickety back screen door slap shut. Then I turned to Star-key and said, 'Gimme the tape.'

"The turtle's little legs started waving frantically as soon as I got close, but it didn't have time to get away. It tucked itself all the way into its shell as we taped the explosive to its midsection. I placed the turtle gently back on the rock, and then Starkey struck the match. There has never been a moment in my entire life when I wanted to do something less than I wanted to take that matchstick from him, but I held out my hand for it. I didn't want to be a pussy, whatever that was, and I definitely didn't want him going after David. He handed me the match, and I lit the fuse. My hand was shaking so hard it took me three tries to get it going, and by then, it was burning my first two fingers. As soon as I saw sparks start flying, I jumped back, dropped the match, and ran a few feet. It was then I noticed Starkey had run several paces and hidden behind a tree. That was the real reason he had needed me—he was afraid that whoever lit the fuse might get blown up. Anyway, my whole body was tensed up like the tightest fist you ever made. I was ready for a huge KABOOM noise. I thought the turtle would completely disintegrate, but it didn't. I wish it had.

"All I heard was a sickening thud, and a sad crack. I almost didn't want to look, but I had to. You know?

"I turned, and there was the turtle, still on the rock, but with a long crack running sideways along the top of its shell. Two or three of its legs were out again, and it was trying to move, but it was only crawling in a little circle. Its head was out, too, and it was looking right at me, like, *Why? Why, man?*

"I knelt down next to it. There was all this wet gooey

shit dripping out around it, and I was wearing newish sandals, but I didn't care right then, you know?

"All of a sudden, Sharkey was right next to me, going, 'Oh, my God. Oh, my God. I just thought he was going to blow up. I didn't think he was going to live!'

"Like it would have been fine if the turtle had just totally blown up.

"I didn't say anything. Mostly because I was crying. Really crying, like with snot running down into my mouth and everything.

"Sharkey said, 'He's looking right at me, man. Shit. Turn his head, Mikey! I just wanted to see what would happen. That's all. I just wanted to see what would happen.'

"The turtle tipped over onto its side a bit, which made things even worse. Now one of its legs was scratching at empty air, and blood was dripping from the raised edge of its shell.

"I couldn't stand it. I picked up the turtle as gently as I could—which was horrible, because I could feel his shell flexing in the middle—and started walking the few steps toward the edge of the water. I thought that maybe if he could get back into the water, he might stand a chance, somehow.

"And if he was back in the pond, we wouldn't have to watch him die.

"Starkey said, 'What are you doing?'

"I said, 'Saving him. He needs to go back in the water.'

"Starkey said, 'No, he needs his shell fixed. I . . . I'll go get some glue!'

"So I put the turtle down in the weeds maybe half a foot from the water, and told Starkey to hurry. He ran home, and I waited. I sat there and sat there. The turtle twitched and whipped his limbs around; my brother eventually started calling for me again; my mother yelled; my brother cried.

"Starkey never came back.

"Finally, when my brother had had breakfast, and the turtle was hardly even moving anymore, I picked it up one more time and pushed it sideways out onto the water. It drifted a few feet, swam a few more, and then went straight to the bottom.

"I stayed there the rest of the morning, until I was starving and sunburned, but that turtle never came back up.

"I think about that all the damn time, man. See, it was easy for Starkey to be a big-ass he-man with his explosives and his threats and his plans, right? And then he made me do the dirty work. But when he saw the actual results, he couldn't face them. All he could say was, 'I just wanted to see what would happen.' And then he ran away.

"And I think that's how this war is going. Can you dig it? These old men in power are making their big plans, and they want to try out their bombs and their tanks and their guns. So they threaten guys like me into going over there and blowing up their turtles for them.

"For what, man? I've already seen how this game plays out. In ten years, or twenty, when they're even older men, they're going to have to see what they've done, and they're going to say, 'I just wanted to see what would happen.'

"Well, fuck that, brother. I ain't playing."

My uncle looked at Jimi and me angrily, almost as though he were daring us to argue with him. But of course, I wasn't going to, and Jimi himself had quit the army. After a long, uncomfortable silence—which wasn't really silent, because the next band, Ten Years After, was wailing away on-stage only a hundred or so feet away—Jimi whipped a huge home-rolled marijuana cigarette out of his pants pocket.

"That's a heavy tale, Michael," he said, lighting and passing the joint. "And the thing is, you have to follow your conscience, you know what I'm saying? Here, let's all have a smoke before my manager declares me dead and keeps my share of the gig fees.

"But do you know what I'm going to do, man? I'm going to give you my guitar after I play in the morning."

Michael coughed out a massive plume of pot smoke. "What?" he asked, choking.

"My guitar, man . . . my white Stratocaster. I've already talked to Gabriel here about it. This guitar was given to me by an old woman in Europe, and it has some unusual . . . you know . . . properties. Gabriel is going to go away for a long time right after I play my set, but you're going to hold on to the guitar for him, all right? And if anything should happen to you, Gabriel will make sure your brother knows this whole story some day. Gabriel said you can't tell David any of this yourself because you're worried about what your parents will do to him. But this way, you'll know that eventually, your brother will understand. All right?"

"But—does this mean—"

Jimi took back the joint from Michael's now-shaking fingers. "Don't think too hard about anything tonight, my friend. You're at the biggest party in history with your brother and your lady, you've got backstage passes, and the evening is young. All this means is that everything will make sense in time, brother. Everything will make sense in time. Right, Gabriel? Your job is to bring the truth home. You've already done it for me. Can you swear you'll do the same for Michael and David if you have to?"

Michael looked confused, but the combination of marijuana, rock-star aura, and three days of Woodstock was hitting him so hard that he actually smiled, reached out, and put his arm around me.

I looked him right in the eye and said, "I promise, no matter how long it takes. If you hold on to the guitar for me, and if you can't tell him yourself, I will make sure that David knows about your draft letter one day."

We shook hands on it, and an electric chill ran through me.

49 BYE-BYES

SUNDAY, AUGUST 17, 1969

Jimi left the trailer to find his band, and Michael and I found our way back to David and our dates. When he saw us, David shouted, "Hey, you missed the greatest guitar solo! There was this English blues band, and they walked right past us when they came offstage. The guitar guy gave Tina his pick—look!"

Tina was jumping up and down with excitement. Debbie kind of rolled her eyes, but then she said, "The band actually was pretty great, I have to say. And guess who's coming on next? The Band!"

"What band?"

"The Band!"

"What band?"

"Theeeeeeee Band. You know, the guys who sing the song that goes, 'I pulled into Nazareth, I was feelin' about half past dead?' They used to be Bob Dylan's backup band?"

"Oh, uh, yeah. Sure, I've heard of those guys. I just didn't know what you meant." I really did know what she was talking about, but it had been a long day, to say the least.

"Anyway, I love them! I hope they play that song. Come sit next to me and tell me all about Jimi Hendrix! Was he as groovy as he looks?"

For a second I almost teased her by pretending to be jealous, but the experience I had just been through was too intense for that, so I said, "Yeah, he really was."

We stood right behind the amplifiers and watched the Band, then somehow ended up lying down on the grass right next to the trailer we had visited backstage for the next two groups, a blues guy named Johnny Winter and a jazzy soul ensemble called Blood, Sweat and Tears. At some point, Jimi Hendrix's management people invited us into the trailer for a late-night buffet feast. I don't know where they managed to get it in the middle of the chaos and darkness, but they had sandwiches, juice, canned soda, and even a fruit tray.

As soon as I took one bite of a turkey sandwich, waves of complete starvation rolled over me, and I gulped down two heaping plates of food like a wolf. I would have been embarrassed in front of the girls, but when I looked up from my fork shoveling, I saw that they were doing the same thing.

"Wow," Tina said around a mouthful of something leafy, "I don't think I've had anything to eat since that cup of granola this morning!" None of the rest of us had, either, but amazingly, I hadn't thought of food once all day.

A guy in a Woodstock staff jacket was standing next to me, and he said, "Only four more bands, man. I can't believe it. I thought this whole thing was gonna fall apart a long time ago, but we've gotten this far. Are you having a good time, buddy?"

That was a hard question to answer. I looked around at Debbie, Tina, David, Willow, and Michael, and said, "I am having an unforgettable time."

He grinned. "That's what I like to hear. Now I have to split. I don't want to miss the next group. They're called Crosby, Stills, and Nash, but they just added a new guy . . . Neil Young from Buffalo Springfield. This is gonna be, like, their first major gig together with the new lineup. Can you imagine playing your first gig with half a million kids watching? It's gonna be a trip! See ya!"

I loved Crosby, Stills, and Nash, so I convinced everybody to finish up their food and come back up the ramp to the stage with me. We crouched down between the amps so we could peek out at the band from the side. Then I felt a tap on my shoulder. Looking up, I expected to see a

Woodstock security person who would tell me we had to get away from the stage. Instead, I found a grinning John Sebastian, who said, "Why are you kids hiding down there, man? Stand up! The view is better, and that way, I can introduce you to some people."

We all jumped to attention and found ourselves facing a lineup of astounding rock royalty. Debbie gripped my arm so hard I thought it might fall off, and hissed in my ear, "Do you know who these people are?"

I did.

For the next hour or so, we stood shoulder to shoulder with John Sebastian, Jimi Hendrix, the guys from Blood, Sweat and Tears, the Band, and Grace Slick from Jefferson Airplane as they all watched in awe. Nobody said much, although at one point, Jerry Garcia from the Grateful Dead offered me a joint. I declined. I wanted to remember every instant of this.

Sometime after five in the morning, Crosby, Stills, Nash, and Young came offstage. When the long ovation died down, and all the congratulations from the rock legends around us ended, we were left in a strangely quiet moment. Debbie pulled me into a little hidden alcove between walls of amplifiers and turned to me. "Gabriel," she said, "you know that whole bubble theory of Tina's?"

"Yeah?"

"Well, I'm trying hard to stick to it. But I just have to say one thing. If I had to meet any one boy in this bubble, I could never have met anyone else as right as you."

She looked incredibly pretty, lit only by the eerie, smoky blue light that made its way backstage. I was so tired and emotionally overloaded that I almost just told her everything then, but I only said, "Debbie, thank you. If I had met you anywhere else, at any other time, I would never—"

She put one finger on my lips and murmured, "Shh. We *are* still in the bubble." Then she pulled me back to where the rest of our group was standing. Willow announced that she was too tired to stay on her feet any longer, so we made our way back down the wooden ramp to the pavilion backstage and sat in a little circle under a tent that had been set up to keep bands' equipment dry. It was really nice to be all together, under a roof, just as the first traces of daylight were beginning to seep into the sky.

Somehow, when we all arranged ourselves, I ended up next to Willow, and everyone else got involved in separate conversations. She put her arm around me, drew me in, and said, "So, do you have any last advice for me, my angel Gabriel?"

"What do you mean?"

"Before you fly back up to the starry skies, silly!" She grinned, but I felt she was only half-joking.

"Um, eat your vegetables? Floss regularly?"

Willow laughed, but then she frowned and stared deeply

into my eyes. "I mean . . . about Michael. Is there something else you came to tell me?"

Hoo boy. I had just been told, emphatically and repeatedly, by the most legendary rock star ever: nothing I said or did was going to save my uncle. On the other hand, now the most beautiful, sad, magical amazing hippie love goddess in the universe was making goo-goo eyes at me and imploring me to open up and tell her what to do.

And, no matter what I had been told, there was something else: Uncle Mike deserved every possible shot. So did Willow. So did my father. Even if it meant that, by saving his happiness, I would be making sure he never *became* my father.

I looked at Willow, took a deep breath, and plunged in. "Listen, there is one other thing. If Michael's plan doesn't work . . . you know, about the draft? If he passes the army physical . . . you have to promise me something. You have to swear you won't let Michael be alone on the night of October seventeenth."

"October seventeenth? Why that night? And how do you know?"

I thought about what Jimi had said, about not ruining whatever happiness my brother and Willow had left. "Please, Willow, I can't tell you. Just swear. October seventeenth. I don't care what you have to do. I don't care what you have to tell him. I don't care if you have to lie. Just don't let him be alone that night. Not even for a minute. I don't care if you have to physically drag him and David to Canada yourself. Just don't let Michael be alone. Will you swear?"

Willow bit her lip, locked eyes with me, and said, "October seventeenth. I swear."

I hadn't known I was holding my breath, but I felt my chest deflate then. Jimi had said that nothing I could do would change what was going to happen, but at least now I would know I had given it my best shot. Or I would never be born, in which case I'd be the world's first nonexistent hero. One or the other.

Willow kissed me on the cheek and whispered, "I will never forget you, Gabriel. Fly safe, okay?" I nodded, suddenly too choked up to speak, and she gave my shoulder one final squeeze before crawling over to sit between Michael and David.

I wiggled sideways a bit and found myself between Tina and Debbie. "What was that about?" Debbie asked.

"Nothing," I said. Then I reconsidered. It didn't seem right to minimize something so huge. "Everything. I was talking to her about Michael. He's so amazing. I feel so lucky that I met him. And David. And Willow."

"And anyone else?" she asked.

I pulled her head to my shoulder, where it fit perfectly into that little area between my neck and my chin. I spoke into her hair. "And you."

A few minutes later, Debbie got up to stretch her legs, and Tina leaned over to me. "Jones," she hissed.

"What?"

"Jones! Debbie's last name is Jones. If you want to look her up when we're all back in the world. Debbie Jones, Astoria High School, Astoria, Queens. Do you want her telephone number? It's—"

"Wait, Tina! What about the bubble? Wasn't that whole thing your idea?"

"Well, yeah, but I didn't think Debbie was going to find true love here. Now do you want her number or not?"

Geez, there was no safe answer to this one. Obviously, I was never going to call, and I didn't want to make Debbie think I would when I was already going to be long gone. "Well," I said, "I know this sounds lame, but I'm not going to be able to call from where I'm going."

Tina's eyes widened. "You mean—you *escaped from prison* to come here?"

For a moment, I thought she was going to start screaming in panic, or hit me over the head with a purse, or something. Instead, she squealed, "That's so *romantic!*" and hugged me. "Don't worry," she said. "I swear I won't rat you out to the fuzz or anything. Your secret is safe with me."

"Wait, I'm not exactly an escaped convict or anything. I just can't—"

"Say no more, Gabriel."

What was I supposed to do? I said no more. Debbie came back, and her head snuggled back under mine. The music washed everything else away, leaving only the bubble around us, for just a little while longer.

We sat there, our heads drooping until we were all kind of leaning on each other, through the entire sets by the next two groups, the Paul Butterfield Blues Band and Sha Na Na. In fact, we might have nodded off completely and slept through Jimi Hendrix's closing set, but thankfully, Tina saved us.

At around eight in the morning, our whole group was basically in a daze, listening to the distant 1950s doo-wop of Sha Na Na, when all of a sudden, Tina started saying over and over, "Guys, I really have to pee!"

Nobody responded for what felt like forever, but finally, David said something like, "Jus' give me a few minutes, Mom."

Then Michael said, "Mom's not here, David. We're at a concert."

That sank into my consciousness, and somewhere in my dazed mind, I remembered seeing footage of Sha Na Na fading into a shot of Jimi Hendrix walking onto the stage. My eyes snapped open, and I started rocking the shoulders of Debbie, who was on my right, and David, who was on my left.

"Everybody, we have to get up!" I said. "Jimi's about to play!"

"And I have to pee!" Tina added.

We scrambled, and by the time Sha Na Na finished their encore, we were all standing by the ramp with Jimi Hendrix and his bandmates. They were all amped up, jittery, and visibly nervous, except Jimi, who just looked lost in thought. He took my arm, leaned his head toward mine so that only I could hear him, and said, "So you were serious about this set? I'm really going to make history today?"

"Absolutely," I replied.

He smiled for a split second, but then frowned. "And you meant everything else you told me? I mean, my father is really going to, you know, be there for me when . . . when my train comes along?"

I looked away, then met Jimi's eyes again. "You still have time, you know. Can't you just, I don't know, be really careful? If you let me tell you what to watch out for, you could—"

"Gabriel, I'm gone already. Please just answer my question. Is my daddy going to help see me home?"

My eyes teared up. "Yes," I managed to say. "Yes, he is."

"All right," Jimi said. Then he turned to his band, put his arms around the shoulders of two of them, and said, "Boys, let's go make some noise!" They all passed around a bottle of red wine as they made their way up the ramp.

We followed the band, but when they went onstage, we circled around the front and jumped down into a little pit area right in front so that we could look up at Jimi as he played. Throughout his set, he kept looking at us, too.

I can't even describe the next two hours, except to say this: I had the best seat at Woodstock. I was with the band. I was with Debbie in our bubble for one more little moment. I was with my uncle Mike for the first and maybe the last time. Plus, I realized, I had spent an entire long weekend with my father—and actually liked him. A lot. Remarkably, his fifteen-year-old self even seemed to like me.

I just hoped I could find a way to keep that going if and when I got back to my "real" life.

Jimi's set at Woodstock was the longest live gig he ever played, but it still seemed to flash by in an instant. Before I was nearly ready, he played the first notes of "The Star-Spangled Banner." "Listen to this," I said to nobody in particular. I didn't have to say anything; the whole place just kind of froze. Watching Jimi Hendrix play that song was like watching someone weave history. When he got to the "bombs bursting in air" part, he somehow made his guitar sound like the Vietnam War. He even threw a phrase from the traditional military funeral song "Taps" in there right before the ending, and you could absolutely feel the mourning spread through the crowd and outward to who-knew-where. But then he finished off the melody with a classical flourish and a rising burst of triumph, so you couldn't help getting a swell of hope for the future, too.

Then he segued right into his biggest hit, "Purple Haze," and again I realized I had been holding my breath without knowing it. The crowd cheered. Jimi looked at me and smiled. Maybe he had been holding his breath, too.

Fifteen minutes later, Woodstock was over. When Jimi and his band finished playing their encore, Michael and I grabbed everyone else's hands and made them rush backstage with us. I was afraid that somehow Jimi might get whisked past us by his managers, and then I would be stuck in 1969 forever, but he made his way straight to me. "You were right, Gabriel. I could feel the power running through the guitar when I played the 'Banner.' Almost like it was playing itself, man! Now, let's plug this thing into an amp and get you home. I . . . I'm pretty wasted. I really have to crash, you know?"

His eyes were incredibly bloodshot. I knew he had been up all night, and I had seen him smoking pot and drinking wine. Plus, who knew what else he had been taking? Thinking about all his talent, and how little time he had left, I just wanted to stand there and cry or something. I must have stood there too long, because he said, "Let's go, Gabriel! We have to do this—before the band splits without me."

Yeah, we had shared some moments, but the guy was still a mega rock star.

Behind his band's amplifiers, there were a few other amps left over from other bands that were still plugged in.

Jimi gestured to my father and my uncle, who were chatting with Jimi's drummer and rhythm guitarist. "I'll tell them you—let's see. I'll say you got a ride out with my manager in a helicopter. All right?"

I wanted to say good-bye properly to Debbie, Tina, Willow, David, and—especially—Michael. But really, nothing I could say was going to make any sense. No matter what I said, the Woodstock bubble was about to pop. My eyes stung as David peered at us between the amplifiers and shouted, "Hey, Mr. Hendrix, can we get a quick picture with you and the guitar?"

Jimi plugged the Strat into one of the amps and said to me, "Now or never, brother. Don't worry, I'll give Michael the guitar, and you'll go tell your father what really went down with his brother."

"My uncle's still going to die, right?"

Jimi said, "It's history, man. I'm history."

"So did I make any difference here?"

"You made a difference for me. Now you have to go back home and make a difference for your *own* self, you know what I'm saying? Come on, now. Play my chord."

And with that, the most famous rock guitarist in history handed me the most famous guitar in history.

I looked over the amps at my father and my uncle one last time. Then I got down on my knees and played that chord.

VOODOO CHILD (SLIGHT RETURN)

TUESDAY, OCTOBER 21, 2014

I woke up in the hospital, with tubes running in and out of me, and immediately had a seizure. The next thing I knew, my father was sitting next to the bed, crying to my mother about Uncle Mike's death. Everything hit me at once then: who I was. Where I was. Where I had been—and what it meant that my father was telling this story.

Jimi had been right. My trip to Woodstock hadn't saved any lives.

"Dad," I said. Well, I tried to say it. My mouth was incredibly dry, my lips were cracked in about a million places, and my vocal cords felt rusted in place. Basically, I said, "Gah."

My mom heard me though, and shrieked. "He said

something! See, I told you he was waking up before. We're right here, Richard. Can you hear me?"

I attempted to make another noise, but my throat had seized up. This was the most warmth I had felt from my mom in years. Truthfully, I felt like bawling.

Dad even piped in. "Can you hear us?"

"Yek."

"Marianne, I think you're right! He did say something. I'll go get somebody."

Classic Dad—fleeing as soon as he might have to interact. I couldn't remember the last time I had actively wanted to be in my father's presence, but this time I didn't want him to go anywhere. We had so much to talk about. I cleared my throat—which was a really painful move—and forced myself to enunciate as I said, "Dad. Stay. Please."

A little bit caveman-esque, but it did the trick. Mom said, "I'll go," and her footsteps tapped their way into the distance.

"What is it, Richard? Is something hurting you? Do you need something?"

Suddenly I was crying, harder than I ever had before in my life. "I'm sorry, Dad," I choked out. "I'm so sorry. I tried. I tried, but I guess I couldn't change anything!" The tears actually lubricated my eyes enough that I could get them open, but I couldn't make anything out at first because (a) I was sobbing too hard, and (b) the whole world was blindingly bright. Eventually, I could make out a shadow looming over me as my father sat on the edge of my bed and put his hand next to mine. He didn't touch me or anything, but he made a somewhat-more-than-half-assed paternal effort.

"Richard," he said softly, "are you talking about the things you said to me on Friday night? Or the damage to the electric guitar? Or the arrest? Or the fire in the basement? We can discuss all of that later. Right now, we have to concentrate on getting you well, all right?"

Fire in the basement? Damage to the electric guitar? I felt another sob course through me. I forced myself to breathe deeply, though, and said, "No, Dad, I'm sorry about Uncle Mike. And Jimi Hendrix. They were both so . . ."

I couldn't even finish. I closed my eyes, and all I could do was picture my father at fifteen, smiling eternally, on-stage with his brother and Jimi.

"What are you talking about, Richie? I know you've been through a lot. In fact, the doctors weren't sure you would even wake up. Maybe you'd better rest a bit. I'm sure your mother will be back any minute with somebody who can help us understand what's going on, and then we can—"

I tried to sit up, but all the wires and tubes stopped me. It hurt. "Dad, you're not listening to me. You never listen to me!"

"What do you mean, Richard? I'm listening, but you're not making any sense. You're talking about your uncle Michael and Jimi Hendrix, but you never met either of them. They both . . . passed away long before you were born. So, um, maybe you had a dream about meeting them? I know you were asking me about your uncle on Friday night, not too long before your . . . accident."

Just then, I had a crazy thought. I closed my eyes again for a moment and tried to concentrate on my right hip. My entire nervous system was beset with pain signals, but I forced myself to wriggle around in bed and attempt to determine whether the hip was still sore. I was fairly sure it was.

"Dad," I said, "I know this sounds crazy, and I know you pretty much think I'm insane half the time anyway. But could you look under the covers at the front of my right hip bone?"

"Richie, why would—"

"Please, Dad. Can you just trust me for once?"

I couldn't tilt my neck down far enough to look at my hip, but I felt cold air as my father pulled the blankets away from my torso. Then he gasped.

"Do you see it?" I asked.

"S-see what?"

"The Cadillac hood ornament?"

"Yes. But—"

"Have you seen a scar like that before?"

"Yes. But—"

"When was the last time you saw this scar, Dad?"

"Umm . . . I—"

"I'll tell you, and you can tell me if I'm right, okay? I think it was August, 1969. I think it was on a kid named Gabriel. I think your brother, Michael, hit him with your father's Cadillac. Check out my hair, Dad. Haven't you been wondering why it's a completely different color now?"

"Richie, I don't know how you know all this, and I don't know when you found the time to put on this . . . this . . . tattoo, or whatever it is. But you should know better than to joke around about Woodstock with me. As for your hair, I'm not sure what you mean about a different color, but it got pretty badly singed when you got electrocuted by the Stratocaster, and what's left isn't really much of a color at all."

Great, I thought. *On top of everything else, my hair is crispy-fried. Whatever. I still have to prove this to my father, or I won't be able to tell him the real reason his brother died.*

But my throat was absolutely killing me. "Can I have a little bit of water, please?" I asked.

"We should probably wait until a doctor says it's all right."

"Come on, Dad. There's something I really have to tell you, and it's waited forty-five years already."

He adopted the father-knows-best smirk that had made me want to strangle him for approximately half my childhood, and I knew my water was not forthcoming. I swallowed whatever meager spit I could force myself to work up, and launched into my big speech, anyway.

"I'm Gabriel."

Dad laughed, a single bark that hit me in the gut like a round of buckshot, but I kept talking.

"Listen. You were in the backseat. Willow and Michael were in front. It was Friday, August fifteenth, and there was music on the radio. I appeared out of nowhere, and the car hit me. I flew into a ditch. Thanks for the clothes, by the way. Does this sound familiar so far?

"You all invited me to come along with you to the festival, so I did. On Friday night, we met Debbie and Tina. Tina was tripping, and she threw up orange juice all over you. Remember?

"On Saturday morning, you and I went down to the pond to wash off, and I'm pretty sure we started the skinny-dipping craze at Woodstock.

"On Saturday night, we accidentally ate some mushrooms and—"

"Richard Gabriel Barber, be quiet for a moment and listen to me! How do you know all this? I haven't told a single living soul about most of it. Your mother doesn't even know about Tina, or the skinny-dipping, or—oh, Lord!—the mushrooms. Did you meet Gabriel somewhere? Has he contacted you over the Internet? I've heard about these Web predators. He didn't seem like the type back when we were teenagers, but then again, I also didn't think he'd disappear for half a century. We met so fast, and then became so close so quickly. He was like my best friend or something, but then he disappeared so suddenly. . . ."

"Behind a wall of amplifiers . . ."

"Behind a wall of . . . Richard, that doesn't prove anything. He could have told you that, too."

"All right, Dad. Why don't you ask me some questions? Things so specific that only Gabriel himself could possibly know the answers?"

Dad nodded slowly. "I still don't believe any of this, Richard. But maybe some questions will help to set the record straight. Who made me a treat for my birthday, and what was the treat?"

"Willow, and it was mushroom brownies."

"Whom did we meet at the nursing tent?"

"The first time or the second time?"

Dad looked surprised for a second, then recovered. "The first time."

"John Sebastian and Janis Joplin. They played 'Me and Bobby McGee' for us, even though her version of it didn't come out on a record until after she was dead."

"What did we have for breakfast on Sunday morning?"

"Easy. Granola, with tea. And you loved the drummer

from Santana the most of all, and you were so excited in the car on the way to the concert that I didn't think you'd ever shut up, but it was really kind of amazing because you never get that excited about anything anymore. We sang 'Dance to the Music' in harmony. You were so . . . alive."

"Richard."

"I'm sorry, but it's true. Anyway, I met such incredible people! You were really nice to Tina. I'm going to miss Debbie. Willow was so beautiful that it almost hurt every time I looked at her. Jimi Hendrix was, I don't know, haunted. And Uncle Mike was the coolest person I've ever met in my life."

Dad turned away from me without a word and walked out of the room. I braced myself for a door slam, but my father surprised me; he just let the door swing shut with a hydraulic hiss. For a few long minutes, I could hear the heels of his shoes clacking past as he paced up and down the hallway.

When I thought I would go insane from either the suspense or my thirst, Dad came quietly back into the room and did something that was an all-time first in our relationship. He put his hand on my shoulder. "This is completely impossible," he said, but it almost sounded as though he was talking to himself. Then he looked me right in the eye and said, "Gabriel? You're really Gabriel?"

I nodded.

We sat there for the longest time, not saying anything, and I kept expecting my mother to come bursting back into the room with an entire medical team in tow before we could finish having this strangest of all interludes. Then I looked past Dad, and saw that Mom was watching silently through the little window from the hallway. I guess even she recognized a moment when she saw one.

Finally, Dad giggled. For a split second, I saw the fifteen-year-old David, high on mushrooms, superimposed on my sixty-year-old father.

"What's so funny?" I asked.

"I just realized something."

"What?"

"Well, when we were trying to come up with a middle name for you, your mother suggested Michael, but I was dead-set against it, because I worried that my brother's name might bring bad luck. So I tried to pick out the name of the one person I had trusted the most, aside from your uncle Mike. In the end, I thought of my old friend Gabriel. So, Richard, as things turned out, I named you after yourself."

LONG TIME
GONE

TUESDAY, OCTOBER 21, 2014

The doctors swarmed over me for a couple of hours, marveling over my miraculous return from vegetable-ville. As far as they knew, most of the damage to my body had been done when I had touched the strings of Jimi's guitar in our basement on Friday night. Dad said sparks had flown everywhere, and I had jerked spasmodically for a few seconds as my hair started smoldering. Then Dad had pulled the plug from the wall, and I had fallen down hard and hit my head on the bare cement floor of the cellar. Nobody was sure whether it was the electricity or the concussion that had rendered me unconscious for the long weekend. I had a feeling my mind had just been . . . elsewhere.

All sorts of medical people came in and ran tests on me. There were blood tests, urine tests, brain wave tests, heart wave tests, breathing tests—it went on and on.

Right before bedtime, my parents left my room. Apparently, they had been taking turns sleeping in a family room on the pediatrics floor, and it was Mom's turn to go home for the night. After they left, one last doctor came by to check on me. I asked him whether he had ever had another patient who had passed out for a bunch of days after an electric shock. He said, "You didn't pass out, Richard. You flatlined. Your higher brain functions stopped. I don't mind telling you, it's a miracle we're having this conversation. So no, I've never had a patient like you before."

"Um, has anyone? I mean, I can't be the only person this has ever happened to. Can I?"

"Strangely enough, I have an old friend from medical school who once told me about a case like yours. I didn't believe him at the time. This case also involved an old guitar amplifier and a teenage boy. Supposedly, the kid found an ancient amp in a warehouse somewhere, plugged a guitar into it, and got a shock like the one that hit you. When he woke up in the hospital several days later, he insisted he had traveled back in time and met the Beatles. Crazy, huh?"

I forced myself to laugh.

He added, "You didn't happen to meet John, Paul, George, and Ringo while you were out, did you, son?"

I managed to eke out another chuckle and said, "No, but I might have hung out with Jimi Hendrix a bit."

"That's a good one," he said. "Sleep tight now."

When he left, I stared at the cracks in the mint-green paint on the ceiling over my bed for the longest time, but even though my body was dog-tired, my mind wouldn't let me sleep. I felt like Jimi and my uncle Mike wouldn't want me to rest until I had told Dad why Uncle Mike had bought and used the heroin. There was a little buzzer on a cord next to my bed for calling the nurse. I pressed it, and when a nurse came in, I asked her to go get my father. I knew he might be mad, because it had to be after midnight, but I also knew he needed to hear what I had to say.

It couldn't have been more than two minutes before my father came barging into the room in a pair of flannel old-man pajamas. My first thought was, *You're wearing those in public?* My second thought was, *Are you going to kill me?* My third thought was, *Showtime!*

"What's wrong?" Dad asked. "Is your head all right? Do I need to call a doctor? Or your mother?"

"No, Dad. I just needed to see you. It's about Uncle Mike. I promised him I'd tell you something."

My father sat down in the chair next to the bed, hard. His hair was matted in seven different directions, his glasses were visibly smudged in the odd fluorescent light, and his face held several days' stubble. It's funny, but you never notice how old and gray your parents look on a day-to-day basis. If you could just spend a weekend with your father's fifteen-year-old self, and then suddenly see him again in his present-day form, believe me, your knees would buckle.

I knew my father was old, but damn.

"This was a secret he couldn't tell you. He told me your parents always took it out on you if you knew he was doing something against their will and didn't tell them about it. Do you remember the time he took twenty dollars out of your father's wallet and came home chewing a piece of bubble gum?"

Dad was staring past me into a shadowed corner of the room.

"Dad?"

"Michael told you about that?"

I nodded. He grimaced.

"I remember. I've never told anybody about that day, but I remember. Our father made me chew that piece of gum all day. I can still *taste* it." Dad's voice sounded like he was gargling rocks.

"Yeah, well . . . so Uncle Mike said if you knew about this one, your father might have really hurt you. He made me swear that if something bad happened to him, then I would tell you the secret. I wanted to tell Uncle Mike it would be a really long time before I would see you again, but there was just no way. Besides, he said this secret would have to wait until either your father was dead, or he was."

Dad sucked air through his clenched teeth and winced as though I had hit him. He was always pretty tense, but I felt like my father might actually crack at any moment. But I had to keep telling him what I knew.

"So I promised—actually, Jimi Hendrix made me promise—that one day I would tell you the truth about this. I don't know why Michael couldn't just trust Willow with it, but it was almost like he thought Willow might not be around anymore, either."

Oh, my God, I thought. *Willow!*

"Dad, what happened to Willow? Did she—" I gulped. "Did she die, too?"

My father sighed and rubbed his eyes. "I don't know. When your uncle passed away, my parents blamed her. She came by the house once, and they had a huge, screaming argument. She left, and I never saw her again. I mean, she completely disappeared—just blew out of town, with no forwarding address. It was a lot easier to do that in those days. I rode my bike over to her parents' house, but they slammed the door in my face, and that was the end of that. I've thought so many times over the years about tracking her down, but . . ."

He let that thought fade, and we sat until I couldn't stand the quiet.

"Dad, remember how Uncle Mike said he was going to take Willow to Woodstock, but then he suddenly changed his mind and got another ticket for you?"

"Yes, of course I do. I've wondered a million times why he changed his mind."

"Well, on Saturday night at Woodstock, Michael and Willow took me for a walk, and he explained the whole thing to me. Dad, your brother got drafted."

"What?"

"For Vietnam. He got drafted, and he didn't want to go. He couldn't stand the thought of hurting anybody. Did you know that about him? There was this turtle."

I had thought Dad looked pale and sickly before, but he was positively green now as he whispered, "Starkey's turtle. With the firecracker."

"That's the one. But he thought you hadn't seen what happened."

"I hadn't, not really. But . . ."

Dad started crying. He wasn't wailing and gnashing his teeth or anything, but tears were definitely making tracks through the stubble.

"But," he continued, "Starkey showed up at the house in an army uniform maybe a week after Mikey died, and told me the whole story. It's so funny how things turn out.

Starkey became a medic in the hundred and first airborne division—said it was because of that day with the turtle. He said that your uncle was the gentlest and bravest kid he had ever met, and that that one day by the pond had turned his whole life around. I remember being scared of Starkey when I was really small, and then after a while, thinking he was all right, but I never knew why he'd changed. How's that for bitter irony? So, if my brother got drafted, why did that make him start using heroin and kill himself? Why didn't he just become a medic like Starkey?"

"Dad, this next part is just going to upset you more. Are you sure you're ready to hear it?"

Dad exhaled sharply. I suddenly realized he had been alternately holding his breath and releasing it throughout this entire conversation. "Richard, *nothing* could upset me more. Go ahead."

"Michael's first thought was to become a conscientious objector, so he said something to your dad, like 'What would you do if I got drafted and became a conscientious objector?' Your dad said, 'I'd rather be the father of a dead soldier than a live coward.'"

Dad looked like he was going to spit on the floor as he said, "Sounds about right."

"So then Willow tried to get Michael to run away with her to Canada, but he wouldn't go because he was afraid of what your parents would do to you if he couldn't come back and protect you. And that was when he came up with his plan. He said he was going to shoot up heroin several times in the weeks leading up to his final induction physical, and when the army saw the track marks in his arm and his general pathetic physical condition, they would reject him. Then he would kick the heroin habit, and get away free without anyone in the family knowing anything about anything.

"I tried to tell Michael and Willow how dangerous the plan was. They snorted heroin on Saturday night, and I could tell it scared Willow. Remember when Michael wouldn't wake up on Sunday morning? But I guess Michael was just so desperate that nothing I said made any difference in the end."

"You know," my father said, "I've wondered every day for the past forty-five years—why that night? Why not sooner? Why not later? I've gone over every second I can remember of my time with my brother, trying to understand whether I did something wrong. Did I hurt his feelings? Should I have noticed some hint? Was he trying to tell me something? Were there clues? Was I a bad brother?"

"Dad, you didn't do anything wrong. Your brother just couldn't see a way out. No matter what he did, he was going to have to disappoint his father, or leave you alone with your parents, or desert Willow. I think he just ran out of options. And I know why he chose that night."

Dad practically lunged at me, his eyes bulging. "Why?"

"I saw the draft letter. His physical was scheduled for Wednesday, October fifteenth, and if he passed, he was due to report for duty on Monday, October twentieth. He must have passed the physical. His time was up."

My father put his head in his hands.

"I'm so sorry," I said. "I know you didn't want to talk about any of this, but I promised Uncle Mike I would tell you everything. I can't imagine how much it must have hurt to hear it, but at least now you know the whole truth, right? So now, after all this time, you know your brother's death had nothing to do with you. It wasn't your fault, Dad."

Dad looked up at me through his interlaced fingers. "Oh, but it was, Rich. Now I know the whole truth. But you don't."

SOUL SACRIFICE

WEDNESDAY, OCTOBER 22, 2014

I t was past two in the morning, forty-five years and four days after his brother's death, when my father finally told a family member the truth about what had happened that night.

"Your mother told you I was on a marching band trip, right?"

I nodded.

"Because that's what I told her. That's what I told my parents at the time, too. It's what I always told them when I wanted to get away on a weekend. But really, I was out with the other guys in our rock band. I figured it all out afterward. . . . Michael sent me away. We used to rehearse in the rhythm guitarist's basement. We always left my drums set up there and everything. On that night, the rhythm guitar player's parents were out of town, so Mike told me we were all going to meet at his house and rehearse some new songs. Then we were supposed to party all night and sleep over.

"At the last minute, Michael backed out. He said he had a special date with Willow. He told me he would drive me over to rehearsal on the way to pick her up, but that I'd have to walk back home in the morning. He gave me ten bucks and told me to take the guys out to the diner for breakfast, relax, give my parents time to wake up before I came home. I didn't even stop to think that was strange. I've wanted to punch myself over and over and over— why wouldn't he have offered to pick me up in the morning? Why didn't that strike me as odd? Why didn't I make a big deal out of it? But truthfully, I was just a little bit excited to be hanging out with the rest of the band without the shadow of my older brother lurking over me.

"So when the time came, I grabbed my drumsticks and my overnight bag—the same mud-stained backpack I had at Woodstock—and jumped in the shotgun seat of Dad's Caddy. Mom and Dad were glued to the television in the living room, beers in hand, so nobody even asked us where we were going.

"I don't remember getting out of the car. It's awful. I don't remember the last time I saw my brother alive. I can recall snatches of the rehearsal, and then somebody brought out the marijuana. When I was really flying, Willow suddenly appeared. She was frantically looking for Michael. She had shown up at our house, and our parents had told her he wasn't around. The bass player kept saying, 'Calm down, baby, he's with you,' and she just kept saying, 'No, his parents said he was with you!' After the fact, I pieced it together that Michael had pulled a fast one on everybody. He'd left the house and told our parents and Willow he was going to be with the band, but he'd told us he was going on a date with Willow. Meanwhile, he had somehow managed to sneak back into his room, as alone as he would ever be.

"Anyway, Willow tried to get me to come looking for my brother, but I was too high. I thought the whole situation was hilarious."

My father stopped talking, got up, paced around the room, got himself a drink of water, took a few sips, paced some more, and continued.

"I'm sorry, Richie. This is hard for me to tell anyone after so long. Willow begged me to come with her. She knew something was wrong. I'm pretty sure she was crying, and she might even have slapped me, but I had to look cool in front of the boys in the band, right? So I just laughed and laughed. Eventually, I blinked a few times, and she was just . . . gone. Then I laughed myself to sleep.

In the morning, I woke up with a sick feeling in my stomach, so I forgot all about taking the guys out for breakfast. Instead, I hurried straight home, let myself in, and tripped over my dead brother. If I had listened to Willow, if I had gone along—who knows? Maybe our first stop would have been my house. Maybe Michael wasn't dead yet at that point. Maybe—"

I felt every muscle in my body clench up. It hurt. I tried as hard as I could to sit up in bed, but all I managed to do was strain my neck forward a bit and make my voice sound more plaintive.

"Dad, you can't *do* this to yourself! Uncle Mike must have wanted to die. He was just a few days away from getting shipped off to the army. He was probably addicted to heroin. His parents were raging alcoholics, and he had no choice but to leave you alone with them. His life was a mess, and he couldn't find any other way out. He gave up."

"But there was another thing, Richie. Something not even Michael knew. Willow had just told me that week, but she was waiting to surprise Michael. In fact, I had been thinking she might tell him that night. In light of what you've just told me, I wonder whether she was waiting until after the army physical to tell him."

"What was it?"

"She told me I was going to be an uncle. Willow was pregnant with my brother's baby."

My head slumped back into the pillow, and a chill ran through me. "Wait a minute. That means I have a forty-five-year-old cousin somewhere?"

"Actually, the child would be forty-four, but of course I have no idea as to what happened, because I didn't track Willow down. That's what haunts me the most."

"You were fifteen. What were you supposed to do? Besides, you said you tried to find her."

"I didn't try very hard, and I didn't stay fifteen. I've had all this time to reach out. What if she never met another man? What if she raised that kid all alone, without any help? What if—"

"Dad, do you remember what Willow looked like? It's not like it would have been hard for her to meet another guy if she wanted to. Plus, you don't know whether she had the baby. But, um, it's never too late to find out, right? The kid would be a grown-up, but I bet Willow would still feel good to know that you turned out all okay, and everything."

Dad looked away from me and mumbled, "Maybe. Maybe. I don't know, though. If I were Willow, I think I would want to spit on anyone I met whose last name was Barber."

I couldn't stand the heaviness, so I made a pathetic attempt to lighten the mood. "So, are there any other horrible secrets you want to get off your chest while you're on a roll? Are you really a top-secret government spy? Is mom not my real mom? Was I abducted by aliens as a baby?"

"There's just one other thing: my Tuesday-night bowling league."

"You really go to strip bars? I knew it! Nobody is that interested in bowling!"

"Ha-ha, Richard. Some respect, please. I'm not your fifteen-year-old pal in the mud at Woodstock anymore."

Ouch. "Um . . ."

"But maybe I can work a little harder on remembering what it felt like to be your age, if you'll agree to work a little harder on being open with me, too."

I didn't say anything. I didn't know *what* to say. But all in all, I was pretty sure my father had just offered me a fair deal.

"Think it over, all right? In the meantime, just listen, because this is important for you to know. A few weeks after your uncle's death, several of our mutual friends took me out on a Saturday night. I know they were trying to do something kind for me, and I suppose in a way, they did. They gave me marijuana, and beer, and pills of some sort. I don't remember many details of that evening, but I do know that I lost all control of myself. The next morning, I awoke in a cell—in the same jail you and I visited a few days ago—with cuts and bruises all over my body, vomit all over my clothes, and the worst headache it has ever been my displeasure to experience.

"The police called my father, who grumbled about having to wake up early to come and get me. The officer in charge knew my parents, and everybody in the precinct probably knew what had happened to my brother, so he let me off with a warning. But my true punishment came a few minutes later. When my father walked in to get me, one of the policemen pointed at me and said to another, 'Chip off the old block, huh?'

"If there is one thing I knew I never, ever wanted to be, it was a chip off the old block. I decided right then and there that I was never going to use drugs or alcohol again."

"What does that have to do with your bowling league?"

"Well, Richie, you've heard of Alcoholics Anonymous, right?"

"Sure. We learned about it in health class."

"When my father and I got home from the police station, I asked him if I could speak with him and my mother. He muttered something sarcastic, lit a cigarette, got himself a cup of coffee, and shouted for her to get her ass down to the kitchen. When she got herself situated with coffee and a cigarette of her own, I asked my parents whether they would consider going to an Alcoholics Anonymous meeting."

"What happened?"

"Your grandfather snorted so hard he choked on his coffee, and then your grandmother said, 'Is this about your brother? Because if it is, let me tell you, a few beers never kilt anybody. If Michael'd had the sense to stick with alcohol, he'd be alive. Hippie drugs might kill you, but a few beers after a day's work ain't no crime. Now you listen here, David: If you don't like the way your parents live, you can just pack on up and get on out. Otherwise, shut your trap.'

"My parents never did get any help, and they both kept on drinking until they died. That's why we never left you alone with them when you were a baby. Anyway . . . I wanted to tell you about my bowling league. There's an offshoot of Alcoholics Anonymous called Al-Anon. It's a support group for family members of alcoholics. A couple of years back, I started having trouble sleeping. Indirectly, it was because of you, I guess."

"Me? What did I do?"

"You didn't do anything. It's just that, when you hit your big growth spurt and started getting serious about the guitar, you suddenly started reminding me so much of your uncle. I began having nightmares about you using drugs, or ending up drunk in a gutter somewhere. You didn't have to do anything—all you had to do was be who you were. My worries did the rest."

"And that was why you didn't let me go out with my friends, or get an electric guitar for so long?"

"A lot of it, yes."

My first impulse was to snap at him. Judging me because I looked like my dead uncle was so unfair. On the other hand, now that I had met Uncle Mike, I got it. My eyes blurred.

I half-whispered, "But Dad, you can't protect me from everything."

"Believe it or not, your mother kept telling me that. But it didn't matter. My anxiety just kept growing and growing. When I couldn't sleep at all anymore, and I thought I might go insane, I asked one of the counselors at work for help. He told me that maybe I should try going to an Al-Anon meeting. I've been going ever since."

"Is it helping?"

"In a way, yes. I've been sleeping better. But there are twelve steps in the program, and I've failed miserably at some of the most important ones."

"What do you mean?"

"As part of the healing process, I'm supposed to admit my wrongs, and make amends to anyone I've harmed. That's been holding me up for a few years now, because I couldn't get past what I did to your uncle. I couldn't save him. Not only that, but when the time came to save him, I was so wasted myself, I didn't even bother trying."

My father got up and refilled his water cup.

"Dad, it wasn't your job to save him. It wasn't even your job to protect him. He spent his whole life trying to protect *you*."

"And failed. Just like I spent my whole life trying to protect you, and failed."

"I'm not going to lie, Dad. Until this weekend, I thought

you were the most overprotective parent in the world, and you're right—that was a pretty massive fail. I hated the way you and mom never let me do anything. But I just realized something else. You did save me, just not the way you think.

"It's pretty amazing that you didn't quit, like Uncle Mike did. So you saved me just by staying alive through all the stuff your parents did to you. Then you didn't do the same stuff to me. So, um, thank you, Dad."

We both got pretty flustered at the straightforward display of appreciation, and my father was so overcome, he needed to take a walk. He was gone for so long that I lost track of time, but the next thing I knew, he walked back into the room and said, "Son, are you awake?"

Truthfully, I wasn't so sure I had been, but I croaked something that sounded like a yes.

"I just realized something. You warned Willow about that *specific* night, didn't you? You told her the date. That's why she was so frantic. I've always wondered, because it was so out of character for her. You warned her in advance, even though saving Michael would have meant you would never be born.

"Am I right, Richie?"

I couldn't answer. My mind was racing, and I felt like something was crushing my chest.

"Am I right?"

"Dad, I . . . yes. I warned her. Jimi told me it wouldn't

make a difference. He told me I couldn't change anything, because it was all already part of my past. But I had to try."

"Why, Richard?"

I couldn't look at my father as I answered. "I don't know. Michael and Willow were amazing people. He was really, uh, noble. You know? And he was my uncle. Plus, you just seemed so happy back then, with your brother. You were just so . . . there. A hundred percent there, every moment. And all the time I've been alive, you haven't been like that. I thought that maybe if I could save Uncle Mike, you could spend your whole life being happy. And all there."

I risked a glance at Dad. His hands were balled into fists and tears streaked his face. "Richard," he said. "You're such a brave boy. And good. Really, really . . . good. I knew it back at Woodstock, when you were Gabriel, but for fifteen years I haven't seen it developing under my nose.

"And I'm sorry. So here is my promise to you. I'm here now."

My father sat back down and put his hand on my shoulder. At some point, we must have both dozed off. When my mom and the first round of doctors came by at sunrise, Dad's hand was still on me. It felt really nice.

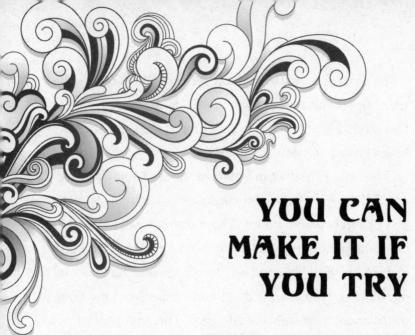

YOU CAN MAKE IT IF YOU TRY

FRIDAY, OCTOBER 24, 2014

They kept me in the hospital for three days "for observation." All of the little burns, scratches, and scrapes on my body healed so fast that one of the doctors told my parents on the third morning that it looked as though they had happened years ago. As for whatever injury had been done to my brain, every medical test had been completely normal ever since I had woken up. The neurologist wanted to keep a close watch on me for a while, and hook me up to some brain scan machines every couple of weeks, but I had a feeling there wasn't going to be anything to see.

The only suspenseful part for me, physically, was what color my still-stubbly hair was going to be when it grew back.

As soon as I walked in the front door of my house, the smell of smoke assaulted my nose, and I bolted for the basement. My parents called after me to wait, but I needed to see how much damage I had done.

The house itself wasn't messed up too badly at all, because the whole basement was mostly made of concrete, and concrete doesn't burn. The burning smell seemed to be coming from my dad's room, so I opened the door, flipped on the light—and gasped. Someone had cleared out all of my father's piled-up mementoes from the floor, so the room itself was basically bare. The entire back wall, the one that adjoined the closet, was singed black, and the closet door was completely charred. I heard footsteps on the stairs behind me, and my dad reached me just as I started walking through the room to see how bad the inside of the closet looked.

"Richie," he said, "it's pretty bad in there. Don't touch anything. We aren't supposed to move anything around until the insurance adjuster has had a chance to inspect the damage."

"Okay. I just have to see what I . . . how bad it is."

"All right."

We walked over to the closet together. Looking in, I saw that the amplifier had burned until it collapsed inward on itself. Jimi's guitar case lay in front of it on the concrete floor, blackened with soot, but looking mostly unharmed. The fabled Strat itself hadn't been so lucky. It was in a corner, with the strings facing up. Apparently, the electricity that had been released when I had played the chord had run along the strings, because the entire fingerboard was charred in six long lines. It even looked as though the strings had melted into the wood in a few spots. Also, the body of the guitar had cracked pretty badly where it had hit the floor as I'd fallen, and the headstock must have banged into either the floor or a wall, because that was broken, too.

I looked at my father and felt tears well up in my eyes. This was a multimillion dollar treasure, and my parents were teachers. It was the most valuable object we were ever going to own, and I had single-handedly trashed it.

We stared for a while, and then my father said, "You know, Michael told me the guitar was dangerous. He warned me that nobody should ever play it but Gabriel. He told me Jimi had said that there was voodoo in it. That's why I tried to warn you."

"Dad . . ."

"Richard, you're going to be grounded for everything that happened Friday night. But I'm not angry with you about the guitar. Really, I'm not. If I had listened to you before you played it, you might have listened to me when I tried to stop you. Besides, nobody would ever have believed us about what this guitar was or where we had gotten it, anyway. I'm just glad you're all right. Houses can be fixed. Sons can't."

"So . . . um . . . what now?"

"Now, Richard Gabriel Barber, you go to your room. And grab your cell phone on the way up. I would imagine you have a few hundred messages from your girlfriend."

"I'm allowed to call her?"

"Well, even prisoners get one phone call, right?"

Forty-five years before, David would have giggled. Now I was pretty sure I saw the corner of his mouth turn up a bit before he said, "Go!"

There was one more thing that I needed to know before I went up; it had been at the back of my mind since the day I had woken up. "One last question, Dad. What was Willow's last name?"

"O'Rourke. Why?"

"Just wondering." I turned and went upstairs before my father could rethink my phone privileges.

Calling Courtney felt strange. Was I supposed to tell her I had cheated? She was the one who always said we were only "seeing each other" when I tried to push for a commitment, so technically, it wasn't like I had done anything against the rules. Besides, she hadn't even been alive yet when it happened. But still . . . Woodstock bubble or no Woodstock bubble, I had gone farther with Debbie than I ever had with Courtney, and that mattered to me.

On yet another hand, if I did tell her I had cheated, when was I going to say it had happened? She had seen me on Friday night, and I had basically been in a coma ever since.

I almost decided to wuss out by texting and saying I was too sick to talk, but when I powered up my phone, I saw that Courtney had sent me more than thirty messages. Thirty messages in seven days, even though she knew I was unconscious for a big chunk of the week—that was a pretty big show of concern. Before I could think too hard and convince myself to stall any further, I called her.

"Rich! You're alive!" she shouted so loudly, I had to pull the phone away from my ear.

"Uh, yeah. I'm fine. I wasn't allowed to call anyone from the hospital, and—"

"You're alive you're alive you're alive you're alive you're alive! Oh, Rich, I thought you were gonna die, and it was all my fault!"

"Wait, why was it all your fault?"

"Your dad didn't tell you?"

"Tell me what?"

"My mom grounded me from my phone and the computer when we got home from jail, right? But then on Saturday morning, the front page of the newspaper had a big headline about your house fire. It said LOCAL TEEN IN COMA, with a picture of you. I freaked, and my mom let me call the hospital. They put me through to your room, and I actually talked to your father. He said the whole thing was his fault, that he had been arguing with you, and then you got so mad that you played an old guitar to get back at him or something . . . and the guitar electrocuted you."

"Yeah, that's pretty much what happened. But it wasn't really his fault. I was the one that lost my temper. Anyway, if it was his fault, how was it your fault?"

"It was the middle of the night after the rally, right?"

"Yeah."

"You were fighting about the rally, weren't you?"

"Yes."

"So it was my fault. I made you play at the rally when you didn't even know what it was for, and then you got arrested, so everything that happened after it was because of me. I'm so sorry, Rich. I would totally understand if you never wanted to see me again. I know you don't even care about politics. I used you just so I could look like an important political organizer person, and then you almost died."

"Courtney, it's okay. I'm glad this all happened."

"You are?"

"I am," I said, and I meant it. I could have done without the parts where I got flash-fried, hit by a huge automobile, and then refried, but other than that, it felt like an experience I had needed. Crazy, huh?

"You know what's weird, Rich?"

"What?"

"This whole week, all I've been able to think about is you. I've been going insane. I can't wait to see you. When are you going to be back in school? I'm thinking maybe we can ditch a few classes, take a walk in the park, and—"

Oh, man. A week before all this, I had always been the

one chasing Courtney around, begging for time. Even hearing her voice brought back how wild she made me feel. But now there was all this stuff about Debbie mixed up inside me, and I didn't know what to do about any of it. "Courtney, listen. You know how you always said we should keep our options open?"

"Yeah, but seeing you up on that stage, watching you get arrested for me, and then hearing about what happened to you in the fire made me realize I was wrong about you. I used to say you weren't a serious person. But you *are* a serious person—and you're the guy I want. What do you say, Richard Gabriel Barber?"

Amazing. I hadn't been called by my full name this many times in one week in my entire life. "Courtney, I think you're beautiful and, um, sexy and you make me crazy. But I have to tell you something. Before you told me all this, there was another girl. And I think you should know—"

"Rich, wait. Does she go to our school?"

"No."

Is she someone I know?"

"No."

"Will I ever meet her?"

"No."

"Will you *ever* see her again?"

"No."

"Are you sure? I mean, do you promise?"

"Absolutely."

"Then please don't tell me anything about her, okay? And I won't tell you about anyone else I might have been seeing before. We can just start over from right now. I mean, if you want to."

"Okay. But I just think we should take it slow. This coma thing was pretty life changing, you know? I'll be back in school on Monday, and I have a study hall fifth period. Would you be up for a walk?"

"Just a walk?"

"Can we see what happens?"

"Rich, if you want me to keep my hands off you completely, you'd better bring a doctor's note."

As you can see, I am excellent at cooling down a relationship.

You know what's funny? Until a week ago, I had wanted to spend every second with Courtney, but she'd said I wasn't ready because I was too "emotionally inexperienced" for her. At the time, I hadn't believed it, but after my Woodstock journey, I understood. More than that—now, I was the one putting the brakes on. After all, we had all the time in the world.

Late that night, I couldn't sleep. I went online and decided to see what I could find out about Willow and

Debbie. I was less nervous about Debbie, so I started by searching for her. All I knew was her age, her name (or at least, her name back in 1969), and where she was from. I looked for Debbie Jones, from Astoria, Queens, born in 1954, and found her high school class newsletter right away. Unfortunately, Astoria High School was huge, and there had been three Debbie Joneses in her graduating class. I searched the archives and found a whole bunch of updates over the years that could have been hers.

If her name was Debra Jones, my Woodstock girlfriend went to Yale, became an accountant, got married in 1977, had three children and seven grandchildren, and was now living happily in Upstate New York in semi-retirement. Upstate New York? Maybe she had fallen in love with the area after the concert, and always wanted to spend more time there? Could be . . .

If her name was Deborah Ann Jones, she graduated high school, got a job as a secretary to the president of a huge investment firm, caught him embezzling money from the firm's clients, testified against him in court in 1983, and became the subject of a major motion picture before entering the Witness Protection Program. She had a husband and two children at the time of her disappearance from the public eye.

Oh, man. If her name was Deborah Sue Jones, she had graduated from Queens College, joined the Peace Corps, helped to feed starving children in Africa for a decade, and never married. On her way home from her last assignment, her plane had crashed over the Atlantic.

There was a section of the site with yearbook photos, but they only went back to the 1980s. I decided that was probably for the best. If my Debbie was Deborah Sue Jones, I didn't want to know.

Then I got to work on the mystery of Willow. It took me about fourteen seconds to locate her. She was on Facebook, which meant that even a technological dolt like my father could have tracked her down if he had ever gotten up the courage to try. Knowing how open she had been back in the day, I figured she wouldn't have restricted any of her info, and I was right. Her friends, her photos, her contact info: It was all out there for everyone to see. She even had links to all of her other online activity, of which there was plenty.

Sixty-three-year-old Willow was a busy lady. She ran an organic gardening business in Maryland. I checked on a mapping website, and found out she only lived three hours from our house. There were hundreds of pictures on her page, and she looked really happy in all of them. She wasn't married, but she had a grown-up son, who had a wife and a daughter of his own.

Her son's name was Gabriel.

EPILOGUE
SPRING 2015

I'm un-grounded. It's been an interesting few months, I must say. Courtney and I have been talking a lot, which I realized we never really did before. I've started playing guitar at some of her political events again, with two major differences: This time, I understand what I am playing for, and so do my parents. Dad got Jimi's Strat restored by a really good local repair guy, and now we have it hanging on a wall in a glass protective case. I have a feeling it's just a regular, old, beat-up, secretly famous guitar now, but we're not going to take the chance that somebody might accidentally play it again.

It's a Sunday, and my father and I have been making time on Sundays for some father-son bonding trips. A few months ago, we drove a couple of hours north of Bethlehem, to the old Woodstock site. Now there's a really cool exhibit hall there called the Museum at Bethel Woods, so we checked that out. Then we walked the fields at Woodstock together. Last month, on the first warm day of the year, we visited Uncle Michael's grave. I spent my own money on a wreath of flowers in the shape of a peace sign. Dad cried. I'm not ashamed to say that I did, too.

On this particular Sunday, Dad has assigned me the very important job of loading up my music player and handling all of the deejaying responsibilities for the journey. As our car approaches the highway on-ramp, I call up my huge playlist of live Woodstock performances and press shuffle. Sly and the Family Stone start up the funky beat to "Everyday People," and I feel like we are back on the way to Woodstock again. But this time, my father takes the ramp heading south.

We're going to Maryland.

ACKNOWLEDGMENTS

This would have been a different, and far lesser, book without the generous and expert assistance of the staff at the Museum at Bethel Woods. Robin E. Green, Assistant to the Museum Director/Registrar, fielded my phone calls and e-mails, dug up obscure historical documents, arranged a private tour, and was just generally awesome to a random stranger who dialed her number one winter day. Site Interpreter Duke Devlin shared his amazing memories of the original Woodstock festival, as well as his insights on fifty years of counterculture history. Security guard Bill Bertholf drove me around town, gave me a detailed account of where all the traffic jams had occurred throughout the festival weekend, and then guided me around the actual concert site (even though it was technically closed for renovations). In a transcendent moment of kindness, Bill even refrained from laughing aloud while I stood where the stage had been and pretended to play a long Carlos Santana guitar solo.

If you are interested in learning more about the Woodstock Music and Art Fair, I highly recommend the Museum at Bethel Woods. The staff members know everything, the site is breathtaking, and the museum itself is a trove. Also, concerts are held onsite throughout the warm months. You can find out more at www.bethelwoodscenter.org.

HISTORICAL NOTE

I have never met any of the real-life characters portrayed in this novel, and anything they say and do within these pages is purely fictional. Also, I did not attend the Woodstock festival. However, I did a lot of research to make the book as realistic as possible. There are a lot of conflicting reports of what happened, both at Woodstock and in the lives of the biggest rock stars of the 1960s. Where sources differ about events onstage and in the crowd at Woodstock, my main guides were Evans and Kingsbury's *Woodstock: Three Days That Rocked the World* (Sterling, 2009), and Gittell's *Woodstock '69: Three Days of Peace, Music, & Medical Care* (Load N Go Press, 2009). Two other fascinating books on Woodstock are festival organizer Michael Lang's *The Road to Woodstock* (Harper-Collins, 2009), and editor Susan Reynolds's compilation of attendees' memories, *Woodstock Revisited* (Adams Media, 2009). In terms of Jimi Hendrix's life and personality, I watched a lot of video and read several biographies.

The text which most informed my portrait of Jimi was Charles R. Cross's gripping, spooky *Room Full of Mirrors* (Hyperion, 2005).

Speaking of spooky, while I initially thought I was making up the stuff about Jimi's guitar and time-traveling voodoo magic, I leave you with a quote from the Grateful Dead's Jerry Garcia, which I only came across when I was already halfway through writing this book:

> *"The thing about Woodstock was that you could feel the presence of invisible time travelers from the future who had come back to see it."*